Trip gathered Charlotte into his arms a_____ **her sha**_____ **one sha**_____

Charlotte_____
nestled u_____
dissipating_____
primal and territorial.

"Trip?" she asked.

"I know. You want to go home."

_____ fingers snuck up to his jaw, and an answering ___ pulsed to that spot. And then she touched his _, lightly dancing over them with her fingertips.

__ly if you're there, too."

JULIE MILLER

PROTECTING PLAIN JANE

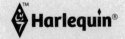

TORONTO NEW YORK LONDON
AMSTERDAM PARIS SYDNEY HAMBURG
STOCKHOLM ATHENS TOKYO MILAN MADRID
PRAGUE WARSAW BUDAPEST AUCKLAND

For all my friends on the www.eHarlequin.com boards and Intrigue Authors Group blog. 2010 was an especially tough year for me, but I truly appreciated all your kind messages and cyber hugs and prayers. Pretty cool. Classy, too. Thank you.

ISBN-13: 978-0-373-74587-6

PROTECTING PLAIN JANE

Copyright © 2011 by Julie Miller

Recycling programs for this product may not exist in your area.

All rights reserved. Except for use in any review, the reproduction or utilization of this work in whole or in part in any form by any electronic, mechanical or other means, now known or hereafter invented, including xerography, photocopying and recording, or in any information storage or retrieval system, is forbidden without the written permission of the publisher, Harlequin Enterprises Limited, 225 Duncan Mill Road, Don Mills, Ontario, Canada M3B 3K9.

This is a work of fiction. Names, characters, places and incidents are either the product of the author's imagination or are used fictitiously, and any resemblance to actual persons, living or dead, business establishments, events or locales is entirely coincidental.

This edition published by arrangement with Harlequin Books S.A.

For questions and comments about the quality of this book please contact us at Customer_eCare@Harlequin.ca.

® and TM are trademarks of the publisher. Trademarks indicated with ® are registered in the United States Patent and Trademark Office, the Canadian Trade Marks Office and in other countries.

www.eHarlequin.com

Printed in U.S.A.

ABOUT THE AUTHOR

Julie Miller attributes her passion for writing romance to all those fairy tales she read growing up, and to shyness. Encouragement from her family to write down all those feelings she couldn't express became a love for the written word. She gets continued support from her fellow members of the Prairieland Romance Writers, where she serves as the resident "grammar goddess." This award-winning author and teacher has published several paranormal romances. Inspired by the likes of Agatha Christie and Encyclopedia Brown, Ms. Miller believes the only thing better than a good mystery is a good romance.

Born and raised in Missouri, she now lives in Nebraska with her husband, son and smiling guard dog, Maxie. Write to Julie at P.O. Box 5162, Grand Island, NE 68802-5162.

Books by Julie Miller

CAST OF CHARACTERS

Joseph Jones, Jr. (aka "Trip")—The big bad giant of a man on KCPD's SWAT Team 1. A wall of well-trained, well-armed protection. He's good with his hands and a heck of a lot smarter than he lets on. His word is his bond. To the death.

Charlotte Mayweather—Kidnapped and tortured as a young woman, this reclusive heiress has a justified fear of strangers. Two friends have been murdered, and someone who knows her darkest nightmares is intent on making her victim number three.

Jackson Mayweather—Charlotte's father. He'll do whatever is necessary to keep his daughter safe.

Kyle Austin—Charlotte's stepbrother. He's all about the family business.

Bailey Austin—Charlotte's stepsister is trying to be a friend.

Landon Turner—This high-school heartthrob was Charlotte's one and only date.

Richard Eames—A trusted family friend.

Jeffrey Beecher—One of Kansas City's most in-demand event planners.

Bud Preston—An employee of Jeffrey's.

Spencer Montgomery—The detective assigned to the Rich Girl murders.

Prologue

The laughter rang in Charlotte's ears and cut through her innocent soul. The muffled music echoing through the school that had filled her with anticipation only moments ago now pounded through her head like a death knell.

"Right. Like I'd go out with some nearsighted brainiac like you when I could have this." Landon, the Prince Charming who'd saved her from coming to the prom with her quiz bowl partner, Donny, leaned over and kissed the raven-haired beauty from the school he'd transferred from earlier in the year. Tears of shock and anger were already blurring Charlotte's vision, but Landon's victorious taunt came through crystal clear. He waved his copy of the prom photo they'd taken a few minutes earlier as proof of their date. "Goal and game for me, sweetheart. I just passed my varsity initiation and earned a hundred bucks, to boot."

Charlotte was shaking beneath the fancy updo of hair that had been straightened and lacquered *within an inch of its life and was supposed to make her look pretty.* "Asking me out was a bet?"

He stuffed the photo into his pocket. "A man's gotta do what a man's gotta do to fit in around here."

And making Charlotte Mayweather, the dateless wonder, think someone special had seen through her plain Jane facade was his way of fitting in? She should have been smarter. None of the other boys she'd had a crush on ever saw her as more than a kid sister or one of the gang. Being smart was the one thing she was really good at. Why hadn't she seen the sham of this boy asking her out? Why couldn't she read people the way she could read a book?

Landon blew her a kiss and grabbed his real date's bottom through her clingy satin dress, letting Charlotte know that while he'd picked her up and brought her to the Sterling Academy's big spring blowout, he had no intention of walking her through those doors into the auditorium and sharing even one dance with her. "All the new guys on the soccer team had a task to complete. You were mine."

Charlotte sniffled and wiped away some of the mascara that was streaking her glasses. "Aren't you the only new guy?"

He shifted back and forth in his black tuxedo, possibly feeling one teeny, tiny iota of remorse. "Hey, *look, Char—nothing's stopping you from going to the dance."*

"By myself?"

"Isn't that how you spend all your nights?"

She took that one like a sucker punch to the gut. She was Charlotte Mayweather, damn it. She had friends. She had scholarships. She had a stellar future traveling the globe in search of historic arti-facts and running her father's museum as soon as she finished Yale and earned her doctorate.

But all she felt was hurt. All she could think of was the betrayal. "You're slime, Landon."

"Yeah, but I just earned my place in your high-falutin' school, I'm starting goalie and I'm gettin' some tonight." He held out his arm for his real date and pushed open the double doors leading to the auditorium. "Let's go, babe."

Charlotte jerked at the instant assault of loud music on her eardrums and got a heartbreaking mental snapshot of the couples and colorful decor inside as the doors drifted shut behind him. She spotted her friend Gretchen floating through the crowd in her tiara, celebrating her win as prom queen. Her best friend Audrey was dancing with Harper Pierce, the tall blond boy she'd had a use-less crush on since they'd been lab partners in chem class. Her homeroom gossip buddy, Valeska Gordeeva, had one guy cutting in on another as they danced.

But when the doors closed and the music muted, Charlotte didn't open them again. As much as she treasured those friendships, she was not going to be a third wheel on anyone's night or humiliate herself any further.

Charlotte tossed in bed, moaning a warning in her sleep as she watched her teenaged self turn and walk toward the school's front door. "Don't go," she murmured, feeling the terror creeping into her nightmare. "Don't."

But after ten years of reliving the same inevitable horror, she still couldn't make it stop.

Charlotte ripped the corsage off her wrist and took one last look at the beautiful red rose and silver ribbons before flinging it to the asphalt and stomping it beneath her foot. "Take that, Landon Turner."

The petty satisfaction of destroying his gift lasted long enough for Charlotte to come up with an even better idea.

"No." She knocked her pillow to the floor, helplessly reaching out in her sleep. "Stay in the moment. Stop."

Pausing long enough to get her bearings in the rows of parked cars, Charlotte pulled off her glasses and furiously wiped away the tears on her cheeks. Ignoring the streaks of makeup left behind, she put them back on and brought her vision and her impromptu scheme into focus. She changed course from her aimless escape and cut through the cars, heading for the opposite end of the parking lot.

The limousine drivers hired for the night—who wanted a family employee ratting to parents about what went on in the back of the car?—were all parked on the far side of the lot, beyond the student cars. She'd find the driver Landon had paid for and have him take her home. Then she'd ask her father to double whatever Landon had paid, maybe send the driver to Vegas for a weekend on the Mayweathers, and Landon and Miss Boobalicious back there could find their own way home.

Charlotte saw the car a couple of rows away, hiked up her gown and hurried her pace. That'd piss him off. Using her first official date with a handsome guy as a joke? He'd be out more than the hundred dollars he'd just—

"Miss Mayweather?"

"Aggh." She pulled up short when the man in the tan coveralls stepped out from behind a car. She clasped her hand over her racing heart. "Yes?"

He swiveled his head back and forth. Was he lost? Looking for someone? "Charlotte Mayweather?"

Tears squeezed between her lashes, steaming against her feverish cheek.

The man faced her again and his fist followed right after.

The blow knocked her to the ground, and her glasses flew beneath the car beside her. Her head was still spinning, her stomach nauseous when she heard the squeal of tires on the pavement and felt the rough hands on her, lifting, dragging. A white van screeched to a halt in front of her. The men who threw her onto the rusty, dirty floor inside were little more than blurs of movement and hurtful hands.

She was scarcely aware of scratching at those hands, kicking, twisting. The blood on her nose was the last thing she saw as a dark hood came down over her head. The slam of a sliding door was the last thing she heard.

The prick of a needle in her arm was the last thing she felt before blessed oblivion claimed her.

"Wake up," she cried into the sleeve of her pajamas, fighting to make the nightmare disappear. "Wake up."

Charlotte woke up to the jarring, concussive sounds of the men beating on pots and pans again. She'd drifted off again. She was losing track of the hour, losing track of the days. Oh, God, they were coming into her room again. "Charlotte! Charlotte!"

They yelled like that to keep her off balance, to keep her from thinking or getting any real sleep, to mess with her head.

"Don't come in." She tried to sit up, but she was too weak to do more than push herself up onto one elbow. She hated when they came in. It was safer when they left her isolated, alone. She was *starving, but she could drink her water and pee without anyone watching.*

The door was opening. They were coming in. She always got hurt when they came in.

"Come on, girlfriend." The one with the big fists from the parking lot threw aside his pan and held up the scissors he'd been banging it with.

"No," she begged when the other two held her down on the bed. "Please, no."

He splayed his hand over her bruised face and turned it into the stale bedding. "I'm tired of waiting for my millions. It's time to show Daddy just how serious we are about the money."

He brushed aside her hair with his long fingers. When she felt the cold metal against her neck, Charlotte screamed.

Charlotte screamed herself awake. She sat up in bed, a cold sweat trickling down the small of her back as she kicked away the covers that had twisted around her legs. She tapped the lamp beside her bed three times, flooding her room with the brightest light possible.

"Max? Stay in the moment," she chanted aloud, repeating one of the mantras her therapist had taught her over the years. Her heart was racing, she couldn't catch her breath. She needed to think. "Max!"

A black-and-tan terrier mix that looked like a miniature German shepherd hopped onto the bed and into her lap. He licked the tears from Charlotte's face as she ran her hands over his short, soft fur, seeking out the grounding realism of the dog's body heat and thumping heart.

Once she was certain she was awake, once her panicked brain truly understood that this was now, not ten years ago—that she was home, not in that smelly beige room—that she was safe—she hugged the dog until he squeaked.

"Sorry, boy." She scratched at his scarred-up ears, kissed the top of his head and pushed him off her lap so she could climb out of bed. "Sorry."

Moving with practiced efficiency, Charlotte picked up the pillow trimmed with Battenburg lace off the floor and tossed it onto her rumpled bed. She pulled her red, narrow-framed glasses from the bedside table and put them on, already heading into the connecting sitting room. She waved her hand in front of the switch there and lit up the crowded oak tables and desk stacked with papers, the bookshelves and antique Americana rugs, the overstuffed sofa and chairs, and went straight to the locks on the door.

While she could visually verify they were all secure, she needed to touch each one—the dead bolt, the doorknob, the chain and the computerized keypad that glowed green to show the high-tech Gallagher Security Company lock was engaged. Once she was certain she was safely locked inside her private rooms at her father's mansion, she spared a rueful thought for her father, stepmother and stepsiblings. Had she wakened anyone on the estate? But just as quickly, she breathed out a sigh of relief. One advantage of living behind soundproof walls was that the same loud noises she wanted to keep out also prevented the rest of the household from hearing her on nights like this one.

After stopping in the bathroom to check the barred window and splash some cool water on her face, Charlotte padded back into her bedroom, pulling aside the thick drapes to check that the locks and laser alarms were still all engaged. Only then did she really stop to breathe. And think.

She hadn't completely wigged out the way she once might have, but she hadn't been able to stop the nightmare, either—a sure sign she was overly fatigued, or more worried than usual about something. Maybe she'd been keeping too many late hours, working at the museum long after closing. Maybe she was feeling like a twenty-seven-year-old imposition to her father and his new wife. Maybe it was agreeing to install the telephone in her quarters after all those years of even refusing to answer one.

The press and police and friends had called around-the-clock. Landon had called her so many times after her release. "I'm sorry. I didn't know. Forgive me," he'd begged. Sometimes, he'd be drunk and would simply say her name, over and over again. The restraining order had finally stopped him.

Maybe it was all those things that had triggered the nightmare again.

Maybe it was nothing.

Max lay over her bare feet as Charlotte looked through the glass and bars up into the night sky. Frothy, fingerling clouds sailed past the full moon and disappeared into a bank of darker clouds, sure signs that a storm was gathering.

She had a sense that something else was coming, too. Something very, very bad.

But in the ten years since she'd been kidnapped and ransomed for five million dollars, she almost always felt that way.

Resigning herself to that reality, Charlotte wiggled her toes to stir Max to his feet and closed the drapes. But the memory of the nightmare—of the real events she'd survived—still sparked through her blood. The notion of sleep, of facing the uncertainty of even the next few hours, took her past her bed and back into the sitting room where she pulled on a pair of white cotton gloves and curled up on the sofa with a box of pottery shards she'd brought home from the museum. She picked up the first piece and a magnifying glass, resuming the painstaking process of identifying and dating the fragments from a dig near Hadrian's Wall in England.

When she got up to retrieve a reference book, she saw the dusty high-school yearbooks on the shelf and briefly wondered why she thought she needed to keep any remembrance from that time in her life. She nodded and headed back to the sofa.

It was because she treasured the past. The now was a frightening thing, the future uncertain. But the past was complete. Done. Finished. Nothing could be changed. There were no more surprises.

She was safe with the past.

It was the present and future she couldn't handle.

Chapter One

Three days later

Charlotte Mayweather eyed the canopy of gray clouds that darkened the Kansas City sky beyond her front door and shivered. She pretended the goose bumps skittering across her skin were in answer to the electricity of the storm simmering in the morning air rather than any trepidation about stepping across that threshold into the world outside.

But with a resolve that was as certain as the promise of the thunder rumbling overhead, she adjusted her glasses at her temples and stretched up on tiptoe to kiss her father. "Bye, Dad. Love you."

Jackson Mayweather's gaze darted to the flashes of lightning that flickered through the thick glass framing each side of the mansion's double front doors. "Are you sure you want to go out in this? Looks like it's going to be another gullywasher."

"You know storms don't bother me." Charlotte cinched her tan raincoat a little more snugly around her waist, leaving the list of things that *did* bother her unspoken. "You can't talk me out of going to the museum. I want to get my hands on those new artifacts from the Cotswolds dirt fort before anyone else does. I have to determine if they're of Roman origin or if they date back to the Celts."

Her trips to the Mayweather Museum's back rooms and storage vaults—where the walls were thick, the entrances limited and locked up tight, and she knew every inch of the layout—were the closest she'd ever come to experiencing an actual archaeological dig. Unpacking crates wasn't as intriguing as sifting real dirt through her fingers and discovering some ancient carved totem or hand-forged metalwork for herself. But it brought more life to her studies in art history and archaeology than the textbooks and computer simulations by which she'd earned her PhD ever could.

It was normal for an archaeologist to be excited by the opportunity to sort and catalogue the twelfth-century artifacts. And it had been ten long years since she'd felt *normal* about anything.

Her father scrunched his craggy features into an indulgent smile. "Those treasures will still be there tomorrow if you want to wait for the storm to pass. Better yet, I can arrange to have them brought here. I do own the museum, remember?"

Thunder smacked the air in answer to the lightning and rattled the glass. Charlotte flinched and her father tightened his grip, no doubt ready to lock her in her rooms if she showed even one glimmer of hesitation about venturing out into a world they both knew held far greater terrors than a simple spring thunderstorm.

Wrapping her arms around his neck, she stole a quick hug before pushing herself away and picking up her leather backpack. *Go, Charlotte. Walk out that door. Do it now.* Or she never would.

She plucked a handful of short curls from beneath the collar of her coat and let them spring back to tickle her mother's daisy clip-on earrings. "I'll be okay." She pulled the check she'd written from her trust fund out of her pocket and waved it in the air. "I'm paying to have those artifacts shipped from England, so I intend to spend as much time as I want studying them."

"I don't like the idea of you being alone."

She zipped the check into the pocket of her backpack. *Alone* was when she felt the safest. There was no one around to surprise her or betray her or torment her. There was no second-guessing about what to say or how she looked. There were no questions to answer, no way to get hurt. *Alone* was her sanctuary.

But he was a dad and she was his daughter, and she figured he'd never stop worrying about her. Still, when he'd fallen in love with and married his second wife just over a year ago, Charlotte had vowed to venture out of her lonely refuge and live her life somewhere closer to normal. Giving her father less reason to worry was the greatest gift she could give him. What years of therapy couldn't accomplish, sheer determination and a loyal friend who'd survived his own traumatic youth would.

"I won't be alone." She put two fingers to her lips and whistled. "Max! Here, boy."

The scrabbling of paws vying for traction on the tile in the kitchen at the back of the house confirmed that there was one someone besides her father in this world she could trust without hesitation.

A furry black-and-tan torpedo shot across the foyer's parquet tiles, circled twice around Charlotte's legs and then, with a snap and point of her fingers, plopped down on his tail beside her foot and leaned against her. She reached down and scratched the wiry fur around his one and a half ears. The missing part that had been surgically docked after a cruel prank had triggered an instant affinity the moment she'd spotted his picture online. "Good boy, Maximus. Have you been mooching scrambled eggs from the cook again?"

The nudge of his head up into her palm seemed to give an affirmative answer.

"Figures," her father added with a grin. "When we rescued him from the shelter, I had no idea I'd be spending more on eggs than dog food." He bent down and petted the dog as well. "But you're worth every penny as long as you keep an eye on our girl, okay?"

Her father's cell phone rang in his pocket and Charlotte instinctively tensed. Unexpected calls were one of those phobias she was working to overcome, but until her father pulled the phone from his suit jacket, checked the number and put it back into his pocket with a shake of his head, Charlotte held her breath. When he offered her a wry smile, she quietly released it. "It's your stepbrother, Kyle."

"You could have taken it. Maybe there's a crisis at the office."

"With Kyle, everything's a crisis. That boy is full of innovative ideas, but sometimes I wonder if he has a head for business."

"Come on, Dad." It was easier to defend the family member who wasn't here than it was to stand up for her own shortcomings. "How long did it take you to learn all the ins and outs of the real estate business? Kyle's only been on the job at JM for a year."

He understood the diversionary tactic as well as she did. "No one is going to think less of you if you decide not to go in to the museum today. I don't want to rush your recovery."

A sudden staccato of raindrops drummed against the porch roof and concrete walkway outside. Clutching both hands around the strap of the pack on her shoulder, Charlotte nodded toward the door.

"I'm fine." Well, fine for her. After ten years of

living as a virtual recluse, she was hardly *rushing* anything by going to the museum today. She caught his left hand in hers and raised it between them, touching her thumb to the sleek gold band that commemorated his marriage to Charlotte's stepmother. "You're moving on with your life. I am, too."

"I don't want anything Laura and I or her children do to make you feel guilty, or push you into something you're not ready for. I know you feel more comfortable at the house—"

"Dad." Charlotte pulled his fingers to her lips and kissed them. "I'm happy for you and Laura. I know Kyle will turn out to be a big help to you at the office and Bailey is, well…" She flicked her fingers through the golden highlights that her stepsister had put in to turn her hair from blah to blond. "We're becoming friends. I've seen you smile more in the past few months than in the ten years since the kidnapping. Think of your marriage as inspiration, not something to apologize for." She released him and retreated a step toward the front door. "My hours may be a little funny, but I'm going to work—just like millions of other people do every day of their lives."

The silver eyebrow arched again. "You're not like other people."

No. She'd seen more, suffered more. She had a right to be wary of the world outside her home. But therapy and a loving parent could take her only so far. At some point, she was going to have to start living her life again.

And stop being a burden to her father.

"There's no miracle happening here, Dad. It's not like I'm going to a party. I'm taking advantage of the museum being closed for the weekend, and this endless weather keeping crowds off the street. I know my driver and don't intend to go anywhere but the car and the back rooms of the Mayweather. I'll be fine once I get to work."

"I can see you've thought it through, then. Are you sure you don't want me to call the security guards in to watch over you?"

Her no was emphatic. "If I don't know them on sight, then—"

"—you don't want them around." His smile looked a little sad that that was one phobia she'd yet to overcome, but she had plenty of reasons to justify her fear of strangers. "Make sure all the doors and windows are locked while you're working—even the doors into the public area of the museum. Double-check everything."

She jingled the ring of keys hooked onto her backpack. "I will."

The front door opened behind her, the wind whooshed in and Charlotte instinctively ducked closer to her father. Just as quickly, she eased the death grip on his jacket and smiled at the retirement-aged chauffeur closing the door. Richard Eames collapsed his umbrella and brushed the moisture off the sleeves of his uniform. "The car is ready, Miss Charlotte. Just a few steps from here to the driveway."

Her father nudged Charlotte toward the man who'd been with the family for more than twenty-five years. "Richard, you take good care of her."

"Yes, sir." Richard took the backpack off her shoulder to carry it for her, then opened the door and umbrella.

For a moment, Charlotte's toes danced inside her high-topped tennis shoes, urging her to run outside the way she once did as a child. It had been years since she'd felt the rain on her face. She lifted her gaze to the dramatic shades of flint and shale in the clouds overhead and breathed in deeply, tempting her senses with the ozone-scented air.

But her father's cell rang again, shutting down the urge.

She clung to Richard's arm while her father took out his phone and sighed. He held up his hand, asking her to wait while he answered. "Yes, Kyle. Uh-huh. Your assistant didn't inform you of the conflict? I see. Of course, the meeting with the accountants is more important. No. I'll handle your mother. You'll report this evening? Good man."

"Is everything okay?" Charlotte asked as he put away the phone.

"Richard." Instead of giving an answer that might

worry her, Jackson turned his attention to the chauffeur. "Clarice Darnell and her assistant Jeffrey Beecher are coming to the house this afternoon to go over the estate layout and setup requirements for Laura's spring garden party and some other events for the company. Kyle was going to handle the meeting, but I'll be taking it now. Be sure to return Charlotte to the private entrance at the back of the house. That way she can go straight to her rooms and avoid our guests."

"I will."

While Richard and her father discussed her trip to and from the museum, Charlotte dropped her gaze from the sky and scanned the grounds outside the white colonial mansion. The trees she'd climbed as a child had been cut down to allow a clear view from the house to the wrought iron fence and gate near the road. She searched the intricate maze of flowers and landscaping her stepmother had put in for any sign of people or movement.

"I saw on the news this morning that some of the creeks south of downtown are closed due to the flooding. Do you have alternate routes planned?"

Richard nodded. "I've been driving in Kansas City going on fifty years now, sir—I think I know my way around. I'll find a dry street to get Miss Charlotte to the museum."

"Good man." Jackson turned to his daughter. "You

have your list of numbers to call if you sense any kind of threat or discomfort?"

"Programmed into my phone and burned into my memory."

Jackson reached down and wrestled the dog for a second before scooting him toward Charlotte. "Keep Max with you at all times, understand?"

"Always do."

"And Richard, I'll double your wage today if you stay with her."

The older gentleman grinned and held out his arm. "I don't charge extra for keeping an eye on our girl, Mr. Mayweather."

Jackson reached out and brushed his fingers against her cheek, as though reluctant to let her out of his sight. It was up to Charlotte to summon a smile and face her fears for both of them. "Bye, Dad."

She set her shoulders, linked her arm through Richard's and took that first step out the door.

The second step wasn't much easier. Nor the third.

With a nervous click of her tongue, she called for Max. The dog bolted ahead and jumped inside the backseat of the BMW as soon as Richard opened the door. She paused, clinging to the roof of the car, fighting the urge to dive in after the dog. "Is he still watching?"

She didn't need to say her father's name. Richard

knew what this brave show was costing her. "He's standing on the porch."

A drop of cool water splashed across her knuckles, momentarily snapping her thoughts from her father and her fears. Almost of their own volition, her fingertips inched toward the drops of rain pooling on the Beamer's roof. How she missed being outside in the—

"Miss Charlotte?" Richard prompted, as the rapid patter on top of the umbrella indicated the real deluge was about to hit.

The impulse to reach out vanished and the paranoia returned. Curling her fingers into her palm, Charlotte climbed in and slid to the middle of the leather seat. Richard set her backpack beside her and closed the door, saluting a promise to her father before shaking off the umbrella and slipping behind the wheel.

Charlotte pushed the manual lock as soon as he was in, even though the automatic locks engaged when he shifted the car into gear. Hugging Max to her side, she turned her nose into his neck. The moisture that clung to his wiry coat was as close as she'd come to feeling the rain on her cheek once more.

Richard found her gaze in the rearview mirror. He smiled like the caring Dutch uncle he was. "Breathe, Miss Charlotte. I know you're leaving the estate for your father's sake, but try to enjoy your day out. The car is secure, my gun is in the glove compartment and I'm driving straight from here to the museum. I'll walk in with you to make sure everything is secure, and I'll wait outside the door until you're ready to come home. I promise you, it's *perfectly safe* to leave the house today."

Perfectly safe. Since that fateful night in high school, perfectly safe had become a foreign concept to her.

The three men who'd abducted her were now in prison, would be for the rest of their lives. But not one of them, not Landon, not the kidnappers, had paid the way she had. Disfigurement. Phobias. Self-imposed isolation.

That night, and the long days that followed, had ended any hope of living a normal life.

Stay in the moment.

This wasn't high school. This wasn't a date. She was older, smarter. She had Max and Richard with her. She'd be all right.

"I'm okay," she insisted, tunneling her fingers into Max's fur. "Drive away so that Dad will get out of the rain."

Richard nodded and pulled away. "Why don't you get out some of those photos and shipping manifests from the museum to distract you while I'm driving?" he suggested. "You'll get lost in your work soon enough."

Giving Max one more pet, inhaling one more

steadying breath, she nodded and reached for her bag. "Good idea, Richard. Thanks. As always, you're a calm voice of reason in my life."

But she crunched the papers in a white-knuckled grip as they drove away from the one place where she *knew* she was safe.

EVEN INSIDE THE PRISTINE atmosphere of the museum's warehouse offices, enough humidity from the rain-soaked air outside had worked its way into Charlotte's hair, taking it from naturally curly to out of control.

She pushed the expanding kinks off her forehead as she straightened from the worktable where she was documenting the artisan's crest burned into the iron hilt of the sword she'd been cleaning. Her back ached, her empty stomach grumbled and Max sat in the workroom doorway staring at her—all certain signs that she'd lost track of the time.

If she'd been at home, more certain of the coded locks protecting her, she might have been grateful that she'd so fully engaged her brain with the task of cataloguing artifacts that she'd actually gone for several hours without her obsessive insecurities dogging every thought. But she wasn't at home. And as she adjusted her glasses at her temple to check her watch, she nearly flew into a panic.

"Why didn't you say something?" She slammed the book she'd been using, startling Max to his feet.

She'd told her father they'd be home by nine, that it was okay for him to go out to dinner with Laura. It was a rare treat for him to enjoy a night out with his wife. The museum was deserted, locked up tight. Charlotte had been in heaven to have the place and all its treasures to herself, *so yes, Dad, enjoy your evening out*.

She slid the sword back into its crate. "It's eight-thirty."

Half an hour past the time Richard was supposed to pick her up. True, he'd been parked in the staff parking lot behind the warehouse all day long, working his puzzles, watching the sports channel on his mini satellite TV, napping. And he'd promptly come to the door each time she'd called him. To walk Max. To bring her lunch. Just to check in and assure herself he was there. If she didn't call him, he knocked on the door. Every hour on the hour.

They hadn't spoken since 7:00 p.m.

Richard was never late.

In a flurry of scattered activity, Charlotte shut down her computer, plucked her raincoat off the back of a chair and shoved her arm into one sleeve. In a miracle of klutzy coordination, she grabbed her bag, pulled out her phone, tutted to the dog and raced him to the steel door that marked the museum's rear exit.

And stopped.

A nervous breath skittered from her lungs. She

couldn't go out there. There was no way to know if it was safe. Evil hid in the shadows at night. Men with fists and needles and greed in their hearts lurked in the dark. They'd lie in wait until it was late and she was alone, and then they'd hurt her. And hurt her. And...

Charlotte squeezed her eyes shut. *Stay in the moment. Stay in the freaking moment!*

"Richard!" She opened her eyes and shouted at the brick walls, even as she pulled out her phone and punched in his number. She tried to focus on getting the other sleeve of her blouse into her coat instead of counting how many times the cell phone rang.

Richard knew how changes in her routine upset her.

That was the third ring. Maybe he'd fallen asleep.

She shifted anxiously on her feet. Four rings.

Charlotte tugged the belt of her coat around her waist and held on as a flash of lightning flickered through the darkness shrouding the unreachable windows above her. Even though she knew it was coming, she winced at the boom of thunder that followed.

Charlotte blinked when she realized her eyes were drying out from staring so hard at the door. Max danced around her feet. "We need to get a peephole installed."

She worked her lower lip between her teeth and reached out to touch the door. The steel was cool from the temperature outside, its texture rough beneath her fingertips. Did she dare open it? Did she risk going outside on her own? She leaned closer and tuned her ears to any sounds of movement in the alley way beyond the door. But a blanket of rain continued to fall outside, drumming against the awning over the door, muffling all but the quickened gasps of her own breathing.

And Max's singsongy growl.

Charlotte's paranoia wasn't fair to the dog's bladder. "I'm sorry, sweetie. Richard?" she called out again, doubting her voice would carry through the steel and bricks and storm to the car parked outside.

The sixth ring.

Max left her side to scratch at the bricks. He whimpered.

What was wrong? Why didn't Richard answer? Her fears multiplied with every single…

The ringing stopped.

"Charlotte."

"Richard? Where are—"

Click.

What the…? He hung on up her? A burst of anger surged through her. He knew what that did to her—how she'd received all those calls and hang-ups in the weeks following the kidnapping. It had taken months of therapy afterward before she'd even allow a phone in her rooms, longer than that to carry one with her.

Richard knew that. He knew… "Oh, my God."

Embarrassment washed away her unkind thoughts, leaving Charlotte's knees weak and her heart racing with concern. What if Richard was hurt? What if he was having a heart attack and needed her help? What if he hadn't called her because he couldn't?

She pocketed the phone and grasped the dead bolt above the doorknob. But her fingers danced over the steel pin, hesitating to grab hold. Could she turn it? Did she dare? Richard had been with her family from the time she was a child. He *was* family. He'd stayed on when he could have retired because she could almost function like a normal person when surrounded by familiar faces, by the handful of staff she trusted. If he'd been driving her the night of her high-school prom, he'd have gotten her safely home. He would never, ever intentionally frighten her.

What if Richard needed her?

Listening to her worries instead of the fear, shutting down her brain and following her heart, Charlotte curled her fingers through Max's collar and turned the bolt.

She nudged the door open, barely wide enough for the dog to stick his muzzle out. Charlotte leaned into the crack until the moisture in the air splashed against her cheek. Max strained against her grip to squeeze through to the gap. "Hold on."

She wasn't ready to do this. She *had* to do this. *Face your fear.*

"Okay." Taking a deep breath and holding it, Charlotte put her left eye to the narrow opening and peeked outside. Her glasses fogged up almost instantly, blinding her. But she pulled the frames away from her face and let the lenses clear. Once she'd readjusted them on her nose, she huffed out a curse at her temerity. She could see the light from the streetlamp at the edge of the parking lot reflected in every rivulet of rain that streaked the polished black fender of Richard's BMW. The car was right there, parked a couple of feet beyond the edge of the green-and-white awning.

Charlotte pushed the door open a few inches more and let Max run out to sniff the rear tire. "Richard?" she shouted through the downpour.

She hurried out to the car. Rain spotted her glasses, distorting her vision before she got the back door open. But Charlotte never climbed inside.

"Are you okay?"

Reprimand gave way to relief. Then her mind seized up with a whole different kind of fear.

She darted around her door and pulled open the driver's door. "Richard!" Her beloved friend was slumped over the steering wheel. "Richard?" Charlotte pulled out her phone, punched in a 9. She swiped the rain from her glasses and glanced around, making sure the narrow lot was still empty, before lightly shaking his shoulder. She punched in a 1. When there was no response, she slid her arm across Richard's chest, her fingers clinging to something warm and sticky at the side of his neck as she pulled him back against the seat. "Oh, my God."

Richard's eyes were open, sightless. Blood oozed from the neat round bullet hole at his temple. She couldn't bear to look at the pulpy mess she'd felt on the other side of his head.

Charlotte.

She jerked her hand away.

Richard never called her anything but "*Miss* Charlotte."

Charlotte whirled around. "Face your fear," she chanted. "Face your fear."

He had her number.

Whoever had done this had taken Richard's cell phone. She'd called him, and now he could call her back.

She shut off the traitorous phone and stuffed it deep into her pocket. She checked every corner and shadow, marked every movement—a car speeding past on the curiously empty street, a wadded-up fast-food sack skipping across the pavement and Max giving chase. "Max…?"

She put her lips together and tried to whistle.

But any fleeting sense of security sputtered out along with the sound. Was there something moving beyond the Dumpster at the end of the alley?

The rain had finally pummeled its way through her thick hair and crept like chilled fingers over her scalp. There were brick walls on three sides of her—three stories high with shuttered windows and iron bars.

And the Dumpster.

"Face…" How could she face what she couldn't see? Her heart raced. Her thoughts scattered. The nightmare surged inside her.

Besides the dog and the dead man, she was alone, right? She saw no one, heard nothing but the wind and rain and her own pulse hammering inside her ears.

But she could feel him. A chill ran straight down her spine.

She caught sight of the blood washing from her stained fingers, dripping down into the puddle at her feet. She snatched her fist back to her chest, her feet already moving, retreating from death and horror and *him*.

Whether the eyes watching her were real or imagined didn't matter. Charlotte's reaction was intense and immediate. Run. Hide. She clicked her tongue. "Max! Come on, boy. Come on."

But the scent of trashy cheeseburger wrappers was too enticing.

"Max!" Operating in a panicked haze, she put her fingers to her lips and blew. The shrill sound pierced the heavy air and diverted the dog's attention. "Get over here!"

Max bounded to her and she scooped him up, yanking open the museum's back door and dumping him inside. Charlotte slammed the door behind her and twisted the dead bolt into place. Oh, God. She hadn't imagined a damn thing. Softer than the pounding of her heart, more menacing than the bloody handprints she'd left on her coat—footsteps crunched on the pavement outside. Running footsteps. Coming closer.

Charlotte grabbed Max by the collar, backed away.

"Charlotte!" A man pounded on the door.

She screamed, stumbled over the dog and went down hard on her rump on the concrete floor.

"Charlotte!"

She didn't know that voice. Didn't know that man.

How did he know her name?

Flashing between nightmares and reality, between Richard's murder and her own terror, the pounding fists seemed to beat against her.

"Charlotte! Come on, girlfriend. I know you're in there!"

They couldn't take her. She'd die before she'd ever let them take her again.

Scrambling to her feet, she scanned her surroundings.

"Shut up," she muttered, trying to drown out the pounding on the door as much as she wanted to drown out the hideous memories.

She wiped her glasses clear. Yes. Safety. Survival.

"Max, come!"

She ran back to the workroom, shoved the top off a wooden crate and pulled out the long, ungainly sword from the packing material inside. The weighty blade clanged against the concrete floor and, for a moment, the pounding stopped.

She pulled out her keys and unlocked one of the storage vaults. "Max!" The dog followed her into the long, narrow room, lined with shelves from floor to ceiling.

"Charlotte! I'm coming for you!"

The banging started up again as she turned on the light and locked the door behind her. He was so angry, so menacing, so cruel. Charlotte crouched against the back shelf, holding the sword in front of her. Max trotted back and propped his paws up against her thigh. The smell of wet dog and her own terror intensified in the close confines of the room. "Stay in the moment," she whispered out loud. She petted her companion, to calm herself, to take control of her scattered thoughts, but stopped when she saw the blood she'd transferred onto the dog's tan fur.

"It's okay," she lied. "It's okay."

But she'd chosen the smart, well-trained dog for

a reason beyond his scarred ear. Max scratched at
Charlotte's coat, nuzzled her pocket. Call someone.
The words were in her head, hiding in some rational
corner of her brain.

"I can't. If I turn on the phone, he'll call me."

We need help.

The deep brown eyes reached out to her, calmed
her.

Charlotte nodded and pulled out her phone. She
couldn't face the police on her own. Couldn't handle
crowds. She turned it on and immediately dialed
the first number her terrified brain could come up
with.

The pounding outside continued, beating deep
into her head. After three rings, a familiar woman's
voice picked up. "Hello? This is Audrey...Kline,"
she whispered in a breathless tone.

"Audrey?"

Pound. Pound.

"Charlotte?" Her friend's tone sharpened, grew
concerned. "Is that you?" A second voice, a man's,
murmured in the background. "Alex, stop. Charlotte,
is something wrong?"

Alex Taylor. Audrey's fiancé. "I'm sorry. I
forget other people have lives. I'll call Dad at the
restaurant—"

"Don't you dare hang up!"

"What is it?" She could hear a difference in

Alex's voice. He, too, sounded efficient, rational, concerned.

"Talk to me, Char."

"I'm at the Mayweather Museum. There's a man at the door. Richard's dead. I can't—"

"Richard's dead?"

The scratch of a dog's paw reminded her to breathe. "Someone shot him and I'm here by myself. There's a man…"

"Alex is calling the police now."

"No."

"But Charlotte—"

"What if it's like…?" Before. Swallow that damn irrational fear. Breathe. "I won't come out unless it's someone I know. Have Alex come."

"We're on our way," Audrey promised, relaying the information to Alex. "Are you safe?"

Alex must be on his phone, now, too. She could hear his clipped, professional tones in the background. "He's not calling 9-1-1, is he? I won't come out for a stranger."

"Shh." Audrey was hushing her, talking to her as if she was the paranoid idiot she fought so hard not to be. "He knows."

"I locked myself inside. Max is with me." Charlotte needed to hear her voice, needed the lifeline to sanity to keep herself from flinching at every pound on that door. "Audrey?"

"Alex is calling a friend of his. Trip's apartment

is close to the museum. We're twenty minutes away, but he can be there in two."

"No. I want you to come."

"Trip's a friend. He's a SWAT cop, like Alex. He helped save my life during the Demetrius Smith trial. He won't let anyone hurt you."

"I haven't met—"

"We're leaving the house now. I don't want you alone any longer than you have to be."

"Wait. How will I know him?"

"Trust me, Char. You can't miss him. He'll be the biggest thing in the room."

The biggest thing in the room? Audrey meant the description to be concise, comforting. But Richard was dead and she was alone, and whoever was banging on the outside door was no small potatoes, either.

The pounding stopped, filling the air with an abrupt silence even more ominous than the deafening noise. Charlotte's breath locked up in her chest. Was he looking for another way to get in?

"Char?"

She jumped at Audrey's voice. "Biggest thing in the room. Right."

"Trip will be right there. The whole SWAT team is on their way."

The instant Charlotte disconnected the call, it rang again. The name and number lit up with terrifying clarity.

Richard's number.

"Oh, God."

It rang. And rang.

"Stop it!"

She pulled her hand back in a fist, intent on hurling the tormenting object against the door. But a paw on her thigh and a glimmer of sanity had her shoving it onto the shelf beside her instead. She'd need it on to know when Audrey got here.

Then she huddled in the darkness with the sword and the ringing and her dog and waited, praying that her friends got to her before whoever had murdered Richard did.

"AUDREY CAN'T RAISE HER on her phone, big guy. You have to go in."

"Got it." Trip Jones stuffed his phone into the pocket of his jeans and peered over the Dumpster into the parking lot behind the Mayweather Museum of Natural History. He pulled his black KCPD ball cap farther down across his forehead to keep the rain out of his eyes, but it didn't make what he was seeing any less unsettling. *What have you gotten me into this time, Taylor?*

Trip retreated a step after his initial recon, wrinkling his nose at the Dumpster's foul smell and running through a mental debate on how he should proceed without the rest of his team on the scene yet to back him up. The rain beating down on the brim of his hat and the metallic bang of an unseen door, swinging open and shut in rhythm with the wind, were the only sounds he could make out, indicating that whatever trouble had happened here had most likely moved on.

Alex and Audrey had lost contact with their friend, and that wasn't good. But he wasn't taking any unnecessary chances. He had to leave the cover of his hiding place and go into that alley. Alone. But he'd go in smart. Flattening himself against the brick wall, he cinched his Kevlar vest more securely around his damp khaki work shirt and pulled his Glock 9 mil from the holster at his waist. He rolled his neck, taking a deep breath and fine-tuning his senses before edging his way around the Dumpster.

Alex had told him three things when he'd called about the off-duty emergency. Find a woman named Charlotte. Keep her safe. And…don't go by your first impression of her. Odd though that last admonition had been, the concern had been real enough to pull Trip away from the book he'd been reading and haul ass over to the museum in the block next to his apartment.

You owe me for this one, shrimp. Trip towered over Alex by more than a foot, and while he might not be quite the tallest man on the force, he was damn well the biggest wall of don't-mess-with-this muscle and specialized training KCPD's premiere SWAT team had to offer. But even he didn't like the looks of what he was walking into. A woman alone at night, in these conditions—something about a murder… Trip frowned. This was all kinds of wrong.

The place was desolate, deserted—solid walls on three sides with bricked-up windows. Rain poured down hard enough to muffle all but the loudest cry for help. A skilled hunter wouldn't have to work hard to isolate and corner his prey here.

And apparently one had.

Trip approached the car at the museum's rear entrance.

Don't be her. Don't be Charlotte. He didn't want to have to explain showing up a couple of minutes too late to Alex and his fiancée. Or his own conscience.

Gripping his gun between both hands, Trip crept alongside the black BMW. He breathed a sigh of relief and cursed all in the same breath. The driver's side doors stood open, the interior lights were on, but no one was home. He put two fingers to the side of the slumping chauffeur's neck. Hard to tell for sure with the cooling temps, but he'd been gone for a couple of hours.

At least the pool of blood was localized. No one else had been hurt at this location. No signs of a struggle in the backseat. But Trip said a quick prayer as he reached in beside the dead man to pop the trunk of the car. After closing the door to preserve what he could of the crime scene, he edged around the back to peek inside. His breath steamed out through his nose.

No body. No Charlotte.

That left the museum's steel door, caught by the wind and thumping against the bricks beneath the awning. After pulling a flashlight from the pocket of his jeans, Trip caught the door and quickly inspected the lock. Scratch marks around the keyhole for the dead bolt indicated forced entry.

He hadn't completed his task yet.

Gritting his teeth and his nerve against whatever he might find on the other side of those bricks, Trip swung the beam of light inside. The museum's warehouse section was dark, with tall, blocklike shapes forming patterns of opaque blackness amongst the shadows. A second sweep led him to the switch box just inside the door.

The electricity had been switched to the off position. The need to move, to act, to fix something, danced across his skin. Dead man aside, someone had broken in and cut the power.

Alex's friend was in serious trouble.

To hell with stealth. "Charlotte Mayweather!"

A rustle of sound answered his echoing voice.

That itch kicked into hyperdrive, pricking up the hairs on his arms and at the back of his neck. "Charlotte!"

Thump.

Perp? Or victim?

He wasn't waiting to find out. "KCPD. Come out with your hands on your head."

He squinted his eyes and flipped on the power switch, creating a shorter recovery time for his vision to adjust as the cavernous interior flooded with light. The shadows became shelves stacked with crates from floor to ceiling, and tables in aisles where more boxes were stored. He swung the light around toward a shuffle of sound and discovered a row of three closed doors marked...

"Not now." He focused the light at the sign on the first door—Z3CVP3 ZTOPVÇ3—and let the letters swirl inside his head until they read SECURE STORAGE.

He didn't have to read the sign on the door to detect the movement behind it. He lowered the beam of light. Another lock. But no signs of entry.

No key, either.

"Charlotte?" He slipped the flashlight into his pocket, tucked his gun into his belt. He jiggled the knob. Sealed tight. He slapped the door with the flat of his hand. "Charlotte!"

Either she couldn't answer or someone was keeping her from answering him.

Trip looked to the right and left, spotted what he wanted and went for it. "Charlotte?" he called out in a booming voice that was sure to carry through the brick walls themselves. He lifted a crate and set it on the floor. "My name's Trip Jones. I'm with

KCPD. I'm a friend of Alex Taylor and his fiancée, Audrey. Are you able to answer me?"

His answer was a soft gasp, the crash of a whole lot of little somethings tumbling down inside that room, a woof and an unladylike curse.

"Charlotte?" The work space around him held a treasure trove of useful gadgets—box cutters, twine, screwdrivers, a drill. He could pop the lock or cut his way in in a matter of minutes.

But the woman might not have that long.

His arm muscles tensed as he set the second crate on top of the first. "I'm comin' in, Charlotte."

Trip tilted the table onto one end, jammed it up beneath the door's hinges and shoved. With one mighty heave, he separated the door from its frame.

The table fell to one side as he pried the busted door open. It shielded him until he could angle around and see into the deep recesses of the closet behind it. "Charl—"

He caught a glimpse of short curly hair and glasses before the woman inside hollered a piercing rebel yell and charged him.

The first blow knocked the door back into him, slamming into his nose and making his head throb.

"Ow!" He tossed the door after the table, held up his hand and reached for his badge so she could see he meant her no harm. "Relax. I'm here to help."

Seriously? Was that a sword? She screamed a

deep, guttural sound that was all instinct and fear. The long metal blade arced through the air.

The blow caught him on the forearm and Trip swore. He felt the sting of the blunt blade splitting the skin beneath his sleeve and knew he had only one option when she raised the archaic weapon again.

Forget reassurances. With a move that was as swift and sure as breathing to him, Trip ducked, catching her wrists and twisting her around. He hugged her back against his chest, lifted her off her feet and shook the sword from her grip. "Damn it, woman, I'm one of the good g—"

He tripped over something small and furry that darted between his legs, and down they went.

Chapter Two

Trip clipped a crate with his elbow on the way down, landing on the unforgiving concrete floor with the panicked woman sprawled on top of him. Thank God he'd broken her fall instead of crashing down on top of her. "Are you okay—?"

"You can't take me!" A swat of thunder echoed her protest and a heel clocked him in the shin, jarring the few bones that hadn't already taken a beating. A dog barked in his ear, lunged at him. Trip swatted it away, but it barked again. The woman he'd come to rescue twisted on top of him, fighting as if *she* was the one who'd just been attacked.

"Sheesh, lady. You're all ri— Scram!" As he pushed the dog out of his face, her fist connected with the gash in his forearm, making the wound throb, and she slipped from his grip. When he felt her knee sliding up his thigh and saw her fingernails flying toward his face, Trip was done playing hero for the night. He caught her wrist, blocked her knee and rolled, pinning both her hands to the concrete above her head and crushing her flailing legs and twisting hips beneath his. "That's enough!"

"Get off me!"

"Miss Mayweather…" Despite the weight of his body, and the unforgiving wall of Kevlar that shielded him from further injury—he hoped—she fought on with futile persistence beneath him. Her funky red glasses flopped across her lips instead of her nose and her exposed eyes were open wide, terrified, like a spooked horse. And hell, it was his fault. "I'm sorr—" But she was still too much of a danger to him to release her outright and let her bang away like the storm outside. "I'm sorry." What he wouldn't give to be armed and built a little less like a tank right now. She was scared and he was probably scarier than whatever had sent her to hide in that room in the first place. "Look, ma'am—"

"No!"

"Hey!" He tried to pierce her terror with his voice. But he was breathing hard, too, and the dog was barking, and he couldn't find the calm tone he needed. "Hey."

"Let me go," she gasped.

"Are you gonna hurt me again?"

Bang. The wind caught the outside door. It slammed into the bricks and every muscle in her body jerked with the sound.

"Richard's dead. He'll kill me this time."

"Lady—"

"Don't kill me." She squeezed her eyes shut, straining against him, tiring.

Trip's blood ran cold. Those were tears on her lashes.

"I'm not gonna… Ah, hell." Shoot him. Make him run ten miles in full gear. Give him paperwork. But do not…do *not* let a woman cry on his watch. "Stop that. I'm not the bad guy here."

"Don't hurt me," she gasped.

He needed to end this. Now.

"Shh. Nobody's gonna hurt you. You're safe. Come on now. There's no need to be cryin' like that." Trip eased himself down, covering her like a blanket with his body, erasing the distance between their chests, controlling her tenacious struggles with his superior size and strength. She'd pass out from exhaustion before he even worked up a sweat at this rate.

"No," she moaned, pushing against his shoulder as soon as he freed her hands. "Please."

"Charlotte, you need to breathe." He brushed a kinky tendril of golden toffee off her cheek and dropped his voice to a husky tone. "Look at me." She shook her head and tears spilled over her cheek, flowing as steadily as the rain outside. "Look at my badge…" Nope, not on his belt. It had gone flying in the initial tumble. She squirmed valiantly, her tired fingers curling into the shoulders she'd pummeled moments earlier. He was desperate to calm her down, to stop those tears, but he wasn't about to go retrieve it with the way she was still writhing so unpredictably beneath him. Ignoring the twinge in his forearm, Trip propped himself up on his elbow and reached for the brim of his cap. She grunted with renewed energy, shoved hard against his chest. "It says KCPD…"

He felt the dog's hot breath in his ear a split second before he felt the pinch on his fingertip. "Ow! Back off, pooch."

"No!"

The mutt was after his hat. "Get out of here!" He wanted to play tug-of-war? Trip closed his fingers around the dog's muzzle and shoved him away. "Give it—"

"Don't hurt my dog!" Charlotte Mayweather pulled her hands away and went suddenly and utterly still beneath him. The mutt pulled the cap from Trip's startled grip and trotted off to a corner. A plea wheezed from the woman's throat. "I'll do whatever you want. Just don't hurt my dog."

She'd refused to give up the fight or listen to reason for her own safety? But she'd surrender for the dog's sake?

Although her golden lashes still glistened with tears, her eyes were suddenly clear, focused and looking right up into Trip's. For several seconds, his vision was filled with deep dove gray. The scents of dampness and dust and heat filled the air between them, filtering into his head with every quick, ragged breath.

For a woman who had as much feisty terrier in her as the dog gnawing on his cap, she'd suddenly gone all quiet, all submissive, all ready to listen to civilized reason now that she mistakenly thought her furry sidekick was going to get hurt. Trip was the one who was bleeding here. Charlotte Mayweather was one seriously twisted-thinking, incomprehensible, crazy...

Woman.

The realization short-circuited the adrenaline still sparking through Trip's body, leaving one sense after another off-kilter with awareness. Curvy hips cradling his thighs. The most basic of scents—soap and rain and musky woman.

And those big, soulful eyes.

"Don't go by your first impression of her," Alex had warned.

Made sense now.

Charlotte Mayweather was a menace to herself and anyone trying to help her. And, while he wouldn't call her beautiful, she was definitely...distracting.

As soon as his conscious brain registered what his banged-up body had already noticed, Trip pushed himself up onto his hands and knees, putting some professional, respectful, much-needed distance between them.

"I didn't hurt the dog," he assured her, swallowing

the growly husk in his deep voice. Yeah, he had a right to defend himself, but his badge didn't give him the right to be making goo-goo eyes at a possible victim or witness. Besides, she wasn't his type. While Trip had never really considered exactly what his type of woman might be, he was pretty sure that pink high-top tennis shoes, flying fists and flaky eccentricities weren't on the list.

He shifted to one side, easing the bulk of his weight off her while keeping a careful eye out for any sign of further attack. "You, I'm not so sure about. Sorry about the takedown, but you forced me to protect myself. Anything bruised up?"

She shoved her glasses back into place, masking her eyes as she scooted just as fast and far across the floor as she could, until the brick wall at her back stopped her. She whistled and the dog jumped up as she pulled her knees to her chest and hugged them tight with one arm. The dog, with Trip's cap locked firmly in his teeth, settled beside her and her free hand drifted down to clench a fistful of fur at the dog's nape. "Did Max bite you? It was an accident, I promise."

"You didn't answer..." Trip crouched where he was a few feet away, keeping close to her level on the floor instead of towering over her and sending her into a freak-out again. Her eyes darted to the black-and-tan dog and back across the warehouse aisle to look at him.

Okay, so she wasn't going to speak rationally about anything besides the fur ball. Fixing a more sympathetic expression onto his features, Trip held up his hand and waved his fingers in the air. "Max, is it? He got a nip in, but I'll survive."

"He didn't mean it. He's not a vicious dog. His job is to keep me from losing it." Um, maybe the pooch needed a little more training? Or was the armed charge and barely controlled panic that moved her body in those rigid, jerky motions her idea of keeping it all together? "He's never been with me when I've been attacked before."

"Hey, I wasn't the one attacking—"

"I don't know if he was defending me, or maybe just wanted to play—but he didn't mean to hurt you."

Trip breathed in through his nose and out through his mouth, forcing himself to relax—wishing she'd do the same. He was guessing she hadn't meant to hurt him, either.

"No harm done." There was barely a blister on the tip of his index finger, but the gash in his forearm was oozing blood through the tear in his sleeve. "On the other hand, I think your sword wound is gonna need a few stitches." He fingered open the rent in his shirt and examined the cut. "You know, I've been stabbed, tasered, shot at—even dislocated my shoulder once on a call. But I've never had to report being brought down by a twenty-pound dog and a broadsword before." Maybe if he kept his voice somewhere short of its natural volume and kept smiling, she'd quit inching up against the wall like that, putting every millimeter of distance between them she could. "Makes you kind of unique."

She didn't so much as blink at the offhand compliment, and offered not even one flicker of a smile at his teasing. "Max weighs twenty-five pounds."

"My apologies." Okay. So he wasn't making any points with Alex's eccentric friend. Better swallow his guilt and stick to police work. Her eyes followed every movement as he plucked his badge from beneath the broken crate, dusted it off and clipped it onto his belt. Trip sank back onto his haunches on his side of the aisle. "Could you at least tell me if any of that blood on your coat is yours?"

Finally giving him a break from that accusatory glare, she glanced down at the stains on her sleeves. With a stiff, almost frantic effort, she rubbed at the reddish-brown spots, turned her hand over to grimace at the slickness that clung to her fingers. With both arms, she pulled the dog up into a hug and choked back a sob. But when her eyes nailed Trip again, there were no tears—only sorrow and distrust. "It's Richard's blood. Maybe yours. I'm not hurt."

"Good." So the woman had been scared spitless, but she hadn't been physically harmed. He was so not the negotiator on his team. Give him something to blow up, break into, fix, and he could handle it just fine. But talking a woman off a mental ledge like the one Charlotte Mayweather was apparently teetering on? Ignoring the tweak at his conscience that *he* had as much to do with putting her on that ledge as her dead friend and an unknown assailant did, Trip focused on the things he *could* handle. He straightened enough to sit on the edge of a table and reached up to his shoulder to tear off his right sleeve. "Did you see the killer? Is that why you were hiding?" He paused midrip. "Ah, hell. You thought I was him, didn't you. Is that why you attacked?"

Her eyes were tracking his movements again. "I know that assaulting a police officer is a really bad thing, but—"

"You have a knack for not answering my questions."

"—to be honest, I didn't know who you were, and after seeing Richard and all the blood, and the noise, and he knew my name—"

"Who knew your name?"

"The man on the phone. The man who called me on Richard's phone. The killer knew my name. He was taunting me." She hugged the dog tighter, and the pooch turned his head to lick her jaw. "He pounded on the door. The calls and the pounding reminded me of…he knows things about me."

"Charlotte…I mean, Miss Mayweather." He'd never seen a person pull herself into such a tight little ball of terror and uncertainty. He didn't understand *pounding* and *calls* and what exactly those meant to her, but he wanted nothing more than to brush those dark gold curls off her cheek, wrap her up in a hug and prove that he was nothing like the man who'd frightened her into such a state. "He won't hurt you," Trip vowed, wisely busying his hands by going back to work on a makeshift bandage by breaking the last threads and peeling the sleeve down his arm. He had a feeling that touching her, or even moving closer, would send her into another panic. "As long as I'm here, nobody is getting to you. And I'm not leaving until Alex Taylor and the people you know and trust get here. Okay?"

After watching her eyes lock on to his without any real relief registering there, Trip looked away to check his watch. Surprisingly, only a few minutes had passed since he'd answered Alex's call—and, he suspected, only a few minutes longer would pass before Alex and the rest of his SWAT team arrived to deal with this off-the-clock rescue. But Miss Hug-the-Dog over there was looking at him as if she'd been sentenced to a night of terror with the beast from some gruesome fairy tale—and he'd been cast in the starring role.

It was hard on a cop's ego, and humbling to any man, to be perceived as the villain—especially when he was used to doing his job and saving the day. He needed the diversion of the pain that made him wince when he pressed the wadded-up fabric against the cut on his forearm to stanch the bleeding there.

The wind outside caught the door again. Trip didn't know if it was the startling noise or him standing that made her eyes widen like saucers. But he figured an apology was useless and strode over to pull it shut.

After wedging a shim of wood between the door and frame to keep it closed, he faced her again. Yep, those suspicious eyes had followed every move he'd made. "Did you know this outside door had been jimmied open?"

"No."

"Then the perp was in here." He perched on the edge of the table again. "You were right to hide. And attack."

"It's not right to hurt somebody else like that." She tucked the swath of curls behind her ear, exposing a flash of a big white-daisy earring. "I'm sorry. I swear I didn't know you were a police officer. I get a little…stuck in my head sometimes."

Trip dabbed at his wound again. "I'm not pressing charges."

"You're not?" She sat up a little straighter, confusion mellowing the distrust on her face for a few moments. But then he could see her gathering her thoughts as she swiped the crystalizing tear streaks off her cheeks. "You're not pressing charges against Max, either, are you?"

"Nope."

"Thank you." A long silence, muffled by the cocoon of rain falling outside, followed as Trip tore off a strip from his sleeve and continued to doctor his wound. Maybe as long as he stayed calm, she would, too. He even thought he saw her hands reach out to help him as he used his teeth to help tie off the pack on his forearm. But as soon as he spotted the gesture, she pulled away and curled her fingers into the dog's fur. "You're Alex Taylor's friend?" she asked instead.

"I work with him at KCPD. We're on SWAT Team One together. Special Weapons and Tactics."

"Alex is…a sweet guy."

"If you say so. I call him *shrimp* when he annoys me. But I can count on him to have my back."

Half a smile curved her full lips. She was testing the option, as if unfamiliar with the idea of relaxing and sharing friendly conversation. "He counts on you, too, I think. He speaks highly of Captain Cutler and your team. I'm friends with Audrey Kline, Alex's fiancée. Audrey is with the district attorney's office. We went to high school together."

"I know the counselor." Trip had a feeling there was no problem with Charlotte Mayweather's mental faculties, but he could see her waging a battle to keep the panic she'd shown earlier from swamping her again. He hoped he didn't say anything that would screw up the tenuous peace between them. "My name's Trip. Don't know if you caught that while you were bustin' up my face and arm."

"Joseph Jones, Jr., Triple J or Trip." If she'd relax just a fraction more, that'd be a real smile. *Please let her smile.* "Audrey told me. And please, it's Charlotte. 'Miss Mayweather' sounds so spinsterish." She touched her slim red glasses on her face. "And I'm already battling that stereotype."

"Thanks…Charlotte. Audrey mentioned you, too. Look, I'm sorry I scared you. If you'd have just answered me…I had no way of knowing if you were stuck inside that closet with the perp—or if you'd been injured. I had to get to you."

She stroked the dog and nodded. "My brain knows that. But sometimes I—"

A cell phone rang in the closet behind Trip, and Charlotte pushed herself straight up that wall. She hugged her arms tight around her waist. It rang again, and he could see any hope of coaxing a real smile or a little trust out of her had passed.

When it rang a third time, Trip was on his feet, digging through the mess in the closet to put a stop to the ringing. Cripes. She'd said the killer had her number. That he'd called to torment her somehow.

He snatched the phone off the floor and answered. "Trip Jones, KCPD. Who is this?"

"Trip? It's Audrey." He could hear the siren on

Alex's truck in the background, heard him on the radio to the other members of their team. "We're a minute away. Did you find Charlotte?"

Trip immediately regretted snapping into the phone. No wonder Charlotte was afraid of him. "I found her. She's…" Unpredictable. Frightened out of her mind. Unexpectedly charming. "…she's safe."

He glanced over to see a woman whose jaw was clenched so tight it trembled. That wasn't right. No one should have to cope with that kind of fear churning inside her.

Trip looked her straight in the eye to reassure her. "It's your friend Audrey."

Although Charlotte nodded her understanding, she didn't say anything until the dog dropped Trip's hat and stretched up on its hind legs, resting a paw against her thigh. Looking down into the dog's tilted face, Charlotte's fingers immediately moved to scratch behind a tattered, scarred-up ear. "Good boy. Mama's fine. Good boy."

What was it about this woman that kept getting under his skin? Guilt that he hadn't gotten the job done he'd been asked to do tonight? Frustration that *he* couldn't make her feel any better, but the dog who'd stolen his hat could?

Or was it something about those haunted gray eyes that triggered all the protective instincts he possessed?

As if she was even interested in being protected by him.

"You can't get here soon enough," Trip admitted, turning back to the phone. "I don't know what to say to her."

"I warned you that she's a little eccentric."

"Yeah, well she's scared enough of me that I don't know if I'm being much help."

The strident sound of a siren, made faint by the building's thick walls, pierced Trip's thoughts. The rhythm of the pulsing sound was different from the siren he could hear over the phone. Or was he hearing both sounds over the connection to Audrey's phone? Wait. He could make out three, five, at least six different siren signals approaching—a lot more than the other members of SWAT Team One could account for.

Audrey was hearing them, too. "Did you call an ambulance? Oh, my God. It's like a parade. Alex?"

Trip tensed, then forced his muscles to relax as he jogged toward the door and pulled it open. "Audrey, put your boyfriend on the phone," he commanded. "Taylor. What's going on? What are you seeing?"

Trip stepped out beneath the awning and spotted the swirls of red and blue lights bouncing off the wall of the building across the alley. Rain pelted his face and streamed down beneath his collar. So much for a low-key response to an *eccentric* friend's call for help.

He recognized Alex's truck turning into the end of the drive and parking at an angle to block the other vehicles. "Looks like we've got more backup than we asked for."

Trip hung up as soon as Alex hopped out of his truck. With his gun drawn, he hurried to the museum's back door, slowing just long enough to catch Audrey by the arm and hurry her on past the limo with the dead driver inside.

"Talk to me, Taylor."

Alex Taylor, wearing the same KCPD SWAT flak vest over jeans and a sweater, shook his head, pushing his auburn-haired fiancée beneath the relative dryness of the awning. "I don't know, big guy. I called Sergeant Delgado and Captain Cutler and that new gal on the team, Murdock. I didn't call the army for backup. Word must have gotten out that it was Jackson Mayweather's daughter who was in trouble. That means the press will be here any minute, too."

"How is she?" Audrey asked, her face wreathed with concern.

Trip felt the heat at his back a split second before he heard the soft husky voice whisper behind him. "What's wrong?"

"Charlotte!"

Trip's impulse to shield the woman taking shelter

behind him was thwarted when Audrey scooted past him and caught Charlotte up in a tight hug. "Oh, honey. I'm so sorry about Richard. Are you okay?"

Charlotte's denial was a quick shake of her head. "It's happening again. It's like before."

"Before what?" But Trip's question went unanswered. Again. Vehicles screeched to a halt out on the street's wet pavement. Car doors opened and closed. There were shouts and a few choice curses.

"What's going on?" Charlotte tipped her chin and blinked against the rain, throwing the question to Trip as if the approaching chaos was all his fault. "Why are all these people here?"

"I'm guessing it's the response to your 9-1-1 call."

"I didn't call anyone but Audrey." Charlotte was hunched over, holding tight to the dog's collar. "I don't want to see anyone. I want to go home." She hid behind Trip as the first uniformed patrol officers dashed around the corner into the alley lot. "I don't like people."

He spun around to keep her in sight. "You don't like people?"

"I don't like strangers. I can't handle people I don't know, especially all at once."

"They're here to help."

"Like you did?"

Ouch. The big gray eyes nailed him with the accusation.

Give it up, Jonesy. You're not going to win this gal over tonight.

"I'm sorry." Apology colored her voice, and she reached out as if she was going to touch him. But she quickly snatched her hand back to her chest. "I shouldn't have said that. All the rumors you've heard about the crazy woman at Mayweather Mansion are true."

"I don't listen to rumors—"

"It's not your fault." The woman was going into panic mode again. "Audrey? What am I going to do?"

"C'mon." Audrey wrapped her arm around Charlotte's shoulders and turned her toward the door. "Let's get you back inside. Alex, keep them away if you can."

"I'll do my best, sweetheart. I'm gonna need you, big guy."

After stowing his Glock back in its holster, Alex squeegeed the rain from his sleek black hair and put up a hand to hold back the officers hurrying toward them. "I'm Alex Taylor, SWAT Team One. The scene is secure, guys."

One of the uniforms kept coming. "Is that your truck? You're gonna have to move it. I've got two ambulances on the scene, with orders to get them in here."

Trip stepped forward, making a bigger blockade. "You need a coroner's wagon, not an ambulance." He nodded toward the BMW. "The vic is an elderly gentleman. Richard...?"

"Eames," Alex supplied the missing info. "Gunshot wound to the head."

The officer glanced inside the car, clearly questioning Trip's authority. "I'll have to check with my superior."

"Do that."

That took care of the first two officers, but the second wave was pulling up at the end of the alley, grouping up to assess and discuss the scene. The response to one frightened woman's call for help was bordering on overkill.

"Just how rich are the Mayweathers?" Trip asked.

"Jackson Mayweather is worth more than you and I both will make in a lifetime—and then some. Once word gets out that his daughter has been harmed again..."

"Again?"

Alex grinned ruefully. "You read all those books and yet you don't know front-page news? Charlotte was kidnapped when she was seventeen. Tortured. Ransomed for millions of dollars. Testifying at her kidnappers' trial was the last time she made an official public appearance. According to Audrey, a situation like this could send Charlotte back into seclusion for…forever, I guess."

Kidnapped? Tortured? Trip felt the blood draining from his head at the memory of him wrestling the terrified woman to the ground. "You didn't think I needed to know that before you sent me over here? I could have done some real harm."

Alex's dark eyes narrowed, surveying Trip from head to toe and back up to his bare arm and the makeshift bandage there. "Maybe we need that bus, after all. What happened?"

"Don't ask."

More people arrived on the scene, this time ranking detectives wearing suits and ties. A pair of EMTs, carrying their boxes of gear, followed close behind. The crew of a news van was already unloading equipment and setting up shots.

Alex's deep breath matched Trip's own. Any chance of secluding Charlotte from the cops and the media was quickly spiraling out of control. "If Charlotte didn't call 9-1-1, who did?"

Trip looked at the phone still clutched in his hand. He remembered Charlotte's instant terror at the idea of the killer calling her again.

"I think I know." Trip lifted his gaze, sweeping the rooftops and bricked-up windows before he advanced to meet the red-haired detective striding toward them. The bastard was still here. The man who'd killed the driver and forced Charlotte to arm herself with an ancient sword was someplace close by—maybe even a part of the frenzy—watching, feeding off her terror. "Get the team on the radio. We need to set up a perimeter."

Chapter Three

He was walking away.

The biggest man in the room, in the whole parking lot, was walking away.

Charlotte pulled away from the hand tugging at her wrist, pushed away the stethoscope sliding beneath her blouse and scooted forward on the gurney to peer through the lingering drizzle of rain to watch Trip Jones rise from the bumper of the second ambulance where he'd been sitting. He smoothed his big palm over the pristine white bandage where he'd been given sutures and a shot. He said something to the paramedic working on him and then turned to follow his commanding officer—a salt-and-pepper-haired man who'd introduced himself as Captain Cutler earlier—over to a meeting of bowed heads and nods with the rest of his SWAT team. Captain Cutler. Trip. Her friend Alex. Another dark-haired man wearing a perpetual scowl. A blonde woman with a ponytail.

Surrounded by a busy anthill of uniformed

officers, detectives, CSIs, reporters, EMTs and family members moving around the museum, alley lot and blocked-off street, her eyes were drawn to the controlled stillness of Trip's SWAT team. Yes, they occasionally glanced around, or turned an ear to their shoulders when a message came over the radios clipped to their flak vests. But they were focused on their own discussion, gesturing occasionally, nodding agreement to one suggestion or another.

Charlotte couldn't explain her fascination with Trip Jones. Although she'd heard Audrey and Alex talk of him, she hadn't met him before tonight. It had been years since she'd met any man who wasn't family or didn't come to the house.

There was something to fear about all that size and strength and specialized training. For one irrational second inside that warehouse, she'd thought he meant to snap Max in two with one hand. Heck, he could have snapped her in two if he'd wanted, and she wasn't any skinny twig of a woman. She hadn't been pressed against that much man and muscle since, well…ever. He'd had every right to get physical with her, but he hadn't hurt her. Although built like a mountain, he was perhaps more like a volcano—a quiet, intimidating presence on the landscape, friendly enough unless all that inherent power in him erupted. Then she could imagine he'd be a far scarier opponent than the man who'd wrestled her to the ground tonight.

Fascinating indeed. She hadn't dated or acknowledged a hormone since the kidnapping. Yet here she was processing an almost intellectual curiosity about a man. One she would most likely never see again.

And who most certainly wouldn't want anything further to do with a screwy piece of work like her.

Charlotte could feel herself disconnecting from the confusion going on inside her head and closing in around her. It was a long-ingrained coping skill—but not the healthiest way of dealing with stress, so she turned away from Trip Jones and struggled to stay engaged with the three men sitting on each side of the gurney and standing with a notepad at the ambulance's open rear door.

Still she longed for her father and Audrey to leave the press interviews they were conducting, to keep the reporters away from her, and take her home.

"Miss Mayweather, I asked if the attacker left you any kind of message." She didn't think it was any accident that the red-haired detective in the suit, tie and raincoat had waved his pen into her line of vision to force her attention back to him. "You were friends with Valeska Gallagher and Gretchen Cosgrove, weren't you?"

He wanted to know about two murdered friends?

Stay in the moment, Charlotte. Engage.

But she couldn't do it alone. She clicked her tongue. "Max. Up here."

Her companion leaped from the damp pavement into the back of the ambulance and crawled up onto the low bed where she sat.

"I went to school with Val and Gretchen." And Audrey Kline and a host of other overachievers at the Sterling Academy. She knew what the detective was asking. "The Rich Girl Killer doesn't murder sweet old men. And no, I haven't received any threatening letters. Richard's killer called me on my phone." She nodded at the plastic evidence bag with her cell sealed inside that Detective Montgomery held. "I think he was trying to find out where I was. He wanted to scare me into revealing myself. He must have read about my kidnapping. He knew..."

She dipped her face down to Max's and welcomed the comforting lick on her jaw.

"Miss Mayweather," one of the EMTs protested the muddy paw prints on the crisp white sheet, "that's hardly sanitary."

The other poked the stethoscope at her again. "If you work with us, this will only take a few minutes longer. Since you refuse to go to the hospital, your father asked us to give you a thorough once-over."

He pulled at Max's collar. She pulled back. "I have a doctor who comes to the house when I need one. I'm fine."

"Miss Mayweather?" The EMT shooed Max outside when she turned her attention back to the detective.

"I've answered enough, Detective Montgomery. I need to go home."

With a nod, he acknowledged the blatant hint to leave her alone, even though his faintly accented voice never wavered from its cool, calm and collected tone. "How can you be certain it was Mr. Eames's killer who called you?"

"I know."

"Would you care to elaborate on how you know that?"

Charlotte smoothed a damp kink of hair off her cheek and tucked it behind her ear. "Would I care…?"

Her ear.

Oh, God.

Charlotte's heart stopped for a split second then raced into overdrive. "Where's my earring?" She tugged at the exposed lobe, scarred and rebuilt from a graft of skin taken from her scalp. Hiding the disfiguring reminder with her hand, she whirled from one EMT to the next. "Did you take my earring? It's a white-enamel daisy. Did you take it?"

She recognized that knowing look exchanged between the two men. "Ma'am, we don't have your earring."

Right. She'd probably lost the keepsake from her mother in the struggle with Officer Jones. She swung her legs off the bed, but strong hands caught her and pulled her back onto the gurney.

"Max? I need Max." The EMT gently took her shoulder and slipped the chilled stethoscope against her skin. Charlotte twisted away.

"We can back-trace the number off your phone."

"To Richard's." She swung her gaze back to Spencer Montgomery. "But you didn't find his cell, did you? I'm telling you the killer took it." She brushed her curls back over her ear to hide the scar. "I want to look for my earring."

"You think the killer took your earring? The Rich Girl Killer takes souvenirs. Did you see him?"

"No. I just…" The panic was taking hold again. She had no keepsake to hide behind, no companion to focus on and keep her thoughts clear.

"Miss Mayweather?" The EMT who'd checked her pupils and pulse dabbed something cold and wet against her arm. When she saw the syringe on the bench beside him, she knocked the alcohol wipe away.

"I don't want any drugs." She put her fingers to her teeth and whistled loudly enough for all three men to pull back for a moment. "Come here, boy."

But the respite was brief.

"Ma'am, clearly you're upset by tonight's events. I need to give you something to calm you. Your heart's racing. We're worried about shock." Max had jumped back inside the ambulance, but the EMT was blocking him from climbing onto the gurney with her. Oh, great. The whistle had caught her dad's attention, too. He was watching her from his press interview, clearly concerned. "Just let me go home. Please."

"We need to remove the dog."

"One more question," Detective Montgomery prodded. "Can you be certain it wasn't your chauffeur calling for help? Perhaps a dying utterance?"

"No!"

"Move it, Fido."

"Max—"

"I need you to lie down."

"Could you identify the voice?"

"No. Please don't." Her mind was spinning, her heart racing. She wanted Max.

"Lie down."

"…hear a gunshot?"

What happened to one more question?

"Give her the sedative."

"I don't want…"

"…identify the killer?"

"Max?"

"The dog stays." The deep-pitched voice silenced the madness, and everything inside Charlotte went suddenly, blessedly still.

The only thing Charlotte could hear was the rain dribbling on the asphalt. The only thing she could see were the broad shoulders of Trip Jones filling the opening at the back of the ambulance.

He looked down at the detective beside him. "This interview is over."

Charlotte's attention danced down to the bandage on his arm, up to the tanned angles of his exposed biceps and triceps. She read the white SWAT emblazoned across his vest, took quick note of the gun and badge on his belt. But in a matter of seconds, before the protests of the three men around her started in, her gaze went back to Trip's grizzled jaw and the green-gold eyes looking down at her with a glimmer of something like intimate knowledge and understanding shining there.

"You're a crazy woman, all right. And I'm not sure I fully understand why. But..." He picked up Max in his arms and set him squarely in her lap. "The dog stays with her."

"Officer, we can't—"

"He's a service animal. With him here you don't need any sedatives. The dog stays."

"We have a job to do."

"You're out of line, Jones."

"With all due respect, Detective, she's been through enough." Trip's eyes cooled and his expression hardened as he looked at Detective Montgomery and the two EMTs, ensuring their cooperation. Charlotte hugged her arms around Max's chest and lowered her chin to the top of his warm, damp head as Trip pulled something from the back of his belt and turned to shout to his friends. "Taylor, let me borrow your cuffs. Sarge? Murdock? Yours, too."

Charlotte watched in fascination as his big hands deftly linked the handcuffs into a long chain. He hooked the last one to Max's collar and placed the jerry-rigged leash into her hand.

"There. Now you can control him and he won't be in anybody's way." As confidently as if they were long-lost friends, he reached out and mussed up Max's fur. "He won't bite." When he pulled away, he winked at Charlotte, startling her, drawing her focus back to his teasing eyes. "As long as you're nice to the lady."

For a moment, her eyes locked on to his. The teasing faded and something warmer, regretful almost, filled the air between them. Unused to her body's curious response to a man who was practically a stranger to her, she hugged her arms tighter around the dog. But she couldn't look away.

Caught up in those eyes, in the kindness he'd unexpectedly shown her, in the confident strength of his presence, she breathed deeply, freely—once, twice. Maybe he was more serene mountain than volatile volcano, after all.

He nodded, breaking the spell. "Charlotte."

And then Trip Jones walked away. Again.

Taking Charlotte's gratitude, and something less familiar and curiously unsettling, with him.

THE MAN SITTING IN THE dark vehicle adjusted the focus on his zoom lens and snapped one more photo, congratulating himself on capturing the image of a bloodied, harried woman, curled into a ball and hugging her dog in the back of an ambulance.

Pleased with his work, he powered down the camera and zipped it neatly into its carrying bag beside the cell phone he'd already crushed beneath his shoe. He tucked the bag into its spot on the floor behind his seat. Then he pulled his computerized notebook into his lap and clicked out of his file of old newspaper files and photos, which had provided all the information he needed to recreate the most vivid, frightening moments in Charlotte Mayweather's life. With two more clicks he was online. He smiled. Yes. People were already chatting and blogging about Charlotte Mayweather coming out of hiding and being involved in another unfortunate incident.

His anonymous post of tonight's events had generated the response he wanted. Just as his helpful phone call had created the crowd of chaos he was enjoying tonight.

Success flowed through his veins as he closed the computer and packed it in its pocket as well. Risking someone spotting the distant glow of his cigarette, he inhaled one last, long drag before pulling it from his lips and putting it out in the ashtray. He crushed the butt down—once, twice, three times before laying it neatly atop the ashes and shutting the tray.

He picked up the gaudy daisy earring from the dashboard and cradled it in his open palm, smiling at the perfect order of things tonight.

A good smoke.

Tidy surroundings.

An unexpected souvenir plucked from the floor of the Mayweather Museum's warehouse.

Yes. She'd just realized it was gone. His old friend was so terrified by his actions that he could see her practically crawling out of her skin as cops and medics and family alike tried to keep her on the gurney in that ambulance. Getting to the reclusive Charlotte Mayweather had been a cakewalk for a man like him.

She'd always thought she had all the answers—that she was smarter, better than him—that her father's money gave her the right to dismiss his talents. She'd made that mistake once—couldn't be bothered with what he had to offer, refused to listen to reason. But he'd proved her wrong tonight. Not only was he intelligent enough to get to Charlotte, he was clever enough to get inside her head.

He breathed in deeply, savoring the lingering smoke in the air, enjoying the satisfaction of a job well done.

Nailing the old man had been simple. All he had to do was walk up and knock on the car window. The chauffeur had actually smiled, perhaps recognizing him, then rolled down the window as if he wanted to offer help. He reached over and stroked the gun and silencer on the seat beside him. The old man *had* helped, had served the necessary purpose. It wasn't the first man's death he'd agreed to in order to make his vengeful plan come to fruition.

He was halfway through his list of wealthy women who'd slighted him over the years. Women he'd once trusted. Women who had used, betrayed and laughed at him. There'd be one more name checked off that list if Audrey Kline's zealous boyfriend hadn't gone into 24/7 bodyguard mode last November. Or maybe it had been his own mistake, thinking he could trust a gang of thugs to follow the rules of his plan.

He bristled where he sat, the sweet aroma of his rare cigarette souring into a foul memory in his nose and lungs. He didn't make mistakes.

His fingers curved around the earring and squeezed, its sharp edges cutting into his skin.

Normally, he preferred to put his hands on his victims, to feel them writhing with fear, to hear them begging for mercy. He opened his hand and forced himself to breathe deeply, recalling Charlotte's screams of terror when he'd beat on the door. The erratic rhythm of his pulse evened out as he replayed her helpless gasp over the phone in his head. He turned from his hidden vantage point and watched her manic movements and pale expression as she dodged reporters and battled with cops and medical personnel amidst the glare of headlights and spotlights and television cameras. Seeing her weakness paraded on display in front of her family and the press strengthened his resolve, calmed him.

This was all going to plan. Charlotte Mayweather craved security, predictability—she needed to know and trust everything and everyone around her in order to function like a normal human being.

He'd take all that and more from her.

Feeling tonight's victory coursing through his veins again, he tucked the earring into his pocket and started the engine. Power over those who had wronged him, control of his own destiny—those were heady things that restored the equilibrium inside his own head.

He pulled onto the street, driving two blocks before turning on his lights and heading across the city.

His thorough research into her kidnapping ordeal, and into the hellish trial that followed, had paid off. He was in her head now, exactly where he wanted to be.

Charlotte Mayweather didn't stand a chance.

Chapter Four

Trip downed the last of his beer in one long swallow and plunked the empty glass on the table. Of all the nights he'd been to the Shamrock Bar, celebrating successful missions with his team, commiserating over the rare loss of a hostage or saluting a fallen friend, he'd always been able to tune out the noise of too many conversations and television sets and concentrate on his friends. Or on a pretty face who didn't mind a little flirtation. Or on one of the classic novels he'd been too frustrated to get through when the rest of his classmates had been reading them back in school.

Thank God for Classic Comics—or he might not have the high-school diploma he'd needed to get into the police academy eleven years ago.

He rolled an imaginary crick from his neck and turned his attention back to the paperback he was reading at the corner table. It might take him all year long, but he was determined to get through the entire *Lord of the Rings* trilogy.

Only, Ents and elves and the scramble of letters he called Mordor kept getting sidetracked by sword-wielding women with pesky dogs and curvy hips and expressive eyes that shouldn't be hidden away behind a pair of glasses.

He turned his page toward the light hanging on the wall beside him and tried to focus. *The qeaçous…* no, *beacons of Gondor are alight, calling for aid.*

But Trip's thoughts weren't in Middle Earth.

The swirling lights and sirens meant backup had arrived. They meant somebody else was here to convince her that he was one of the good guys. "They're here to help."

"Like you did?"

Trip's gaze drifted to the blank margin at the bottom of the page. Where did Charlotte Mayweather get off, all but accusing him of making a horrible night even worse for her? He'd volunteered on his own time to check on the friend of a friend in need. The dead body and forced lock he'd found had put him on full-alert-combat mode. The woman was safe with him there. She didn't need to be afraid or cry or go psycho on him.

She just needed to believe that he'd protect her—at any cost—because that was his job. It was who he was. It was what six feet, five inches of brawn, resourceful instincts and a talented set of hands was best suited for. He'd told her as much—had shown her—but she still didn't believe he was one of the good guys.

And then she'd cried on him? The stitches in his arm and threat of a killer on the loose he could handle. But those tears trickling over her cheeks had twisted his stomach into a knot and made him useless to her.

And why was that stunned feeling of incompetence the memory that niggled his conscience two nights after the fact? Why wasn't he analyzing the syrupy heat that had stirred in his veins when she'd halfway smiled at him for answering her tomboy whistle and plopping the dog in her lap?

Why was anything at all about Charlotte Mayweather still stuck in his head?

Trip closed his book and reached for his empty glass, tuning in to the other people in the bar. Captain Cutler sat at the end of the table, reading over the report from their performance-evaluation drill this afternoon. Alex Taylor sat directly across from him, on the phone with Audrey. Rafe Delgado was up at the bar, leaning in to stand nose-to-nose with their favorite bartender and adopted little sister, Josie Nichols.

Whatever that hushed argument was about, Josie was standing her ground, flipping her long dark ponytail behind her back and tilting her chin, despite the fatigue that was evident in her posture. For half a moment, Trip considered poking his nose in and warning Sergeant Delgado to back it up a step. Couldn't he see how she braced her hands at the small of her back? The woman was dead on her feet, attending nursing school by day and working long hours at her uncle's bar at night. She didn't need whatever grief Rafe was giving her right now. But then Trip's rescuing skills seemed to be a little on the fritz right now.

Still, Rafe seemed to be taking his overprotective-big-brother thing with Josie a little too far. Since she was the daughter of his first partner, who'd been killed in the line of duty, there was probably a stronger connection there. But it turned out there was no need to intervene. Josie flattened her hand in the middle of the sergeant's chest and pushed him out of her space before spinning around and returning to her duties behind the bar.

Seemed like Charlotte Mayweather wasn't the only woman who didn't want SWAT Team One looking out for her.

"Here we go." Randy Murdock, the newest member of the team, was driven and talented and female. *Miranda,* a feminine name that didn't seem to fit either her personality or her deadly aim with a Remington sniper rifle, set a tray of beers on the table. The unwritten law was that the new guy bought the second round of drinks, since Josie Nichols seemed to always find an excuse to serve their first drinks on the house. "Everyone wanted a draft, right?"

"Works for me." Trip reached across the table and picked up his second beer. He wouldn't resort to getting drunk to get his frustration with a certain toffee-haired heiress out of his system, but getting his hands busy with something else might. "Thanks, newbie."

Randy slid into the chair beside Trip's, pulling a beer in front of her, too. "I don't want you guys to think that just because I'm the only woman on the team that I'm going to be serving the drinks all the time. And don't expect me to bake brownies or darn your socks."

"Don't expect me to darn yours, either," Trip teased, appreciating the normal interaction with a woman.

"You can sew?" she countered.

"You can cook?"

The blonde's cheeks blossomed with a blush that she quickly hid behind a swig of her beer.

"Down, you two." Captain Cutler chided them like a stern father, setting the report down on the table and picking up a glass. His dark blue eyes zeroed in on Randy. "As long as you keep making a perfect score on the target range, you don't have to bring me another beer."

"I don't mind doing that for you, sir."

Michael Cutler grinned. "Relax, Murdock—I'm

paying you a compliment. Team One's score today was the highest ever recorded on the course. Captain Sanchez on Team Two owes me twenty bucks. And I intend to collect."

"Congratulations, sir."

"Congratulations to my team." Cutler raised his glass and signaled to Sergeant Delgado to come over to the table and join their toast. "Now, you all perform that well on the street, and I can rest easy when I go home to my wife at night."

Trip raised his glass and took a drink to honor his team's performance on the mock-terrorist-attack drill this afternoon. Even during those lucky stretches of time when there was no real bomb threat or fugitive alert or hostage crisis that needed SWAT on the scene, they trained in weapons and strategy to keep their skills and instincts sharp. Today's drill had gone by the book—full cooperation, each playing to his or her strength, no mistakes.

So why couldn't he be savoring that victory instead of stewing over some eccentric kook…?

Trip's gaze skidded to the neat shock of red hair on the man walking through the Shamrock's front door. One thing about hanging out at a cop bar was that eventually, almost every cop in KCPD, active or retired, would stop by. Even the ones he didn't particularly like. Trip barely knew Spencer Montgomery, but something about a detective relentlessly badgering a witness in an ambulance when it was plain to anybody who looked that she was about to lose it, put him on Trip's don't-turn-your-back-on-him-yet list.

Detective Montgomery must have felt Trip's eyes on him because he paused before sitting and turned, trading nods of acknowledgment, if no smile of kinship, with him. Montgomery and his dark-haired partner had been assigned to the Rich Girl Killer investigation. A serial killer had already tortured and strangled two of Kansas City's wealthiest beauties and was believed to be responsible for one or two more unsolved deaths. Just last year the killer had targeted Alex's fiancée, but the perp had eluded identification and gone underground. Did Montgomery think there was some kind of connection between the dead chauffeur and the murderer he was after?

Trip sat up straight in his chair.

Was *that* the killer Charlotte Mayweather feared?

The man she'd thought *he* was?

Maybe the prickly heiress's paranoia wasn't all about the trauma of being kidnapped ten years ago.

"All right, sweetheart, I'll see what I can do. You will *not*. You will not." Alex's voice interrupted Trip's silent speculation. "If that's the case, it's not up for negotiation. As soon as I'm done here, I'll swing by to pick you up."

"Problems with the soon-to-be missus?" Trip

felt he'd better make a comment before anyone noticed his unusual preoccupation with his thoughts tonight.

"Just a little discussion about taking unnecessary risks." Alex closed his phone and slipped it into the pocket of his jeans. "We reached a compromise."

"She'll go ahead and do what she wants and you won't complain about it?"

"Ha-ha, big guy. I wouldn't be giving me too much grief. You've been all kinds of quiet since that night at the Mayweather Museum." So his brooding hadn't gone unnoticed. "On the other hand, whatever you said or did, Charlotte's still talking about it. Audrey's at her house right now."

"Is she filing a harassment claim with the D.A.'s office?"

"Not exactly."

"What *exactly* is she saying about me?"

Captain Cutler put an end to the conversation. "What is this, junior high? You two settle your love lives on your own time. I just won a bet."

"Congratulations, captain," Alex took a drink and then pushed his glass away. "Sorry to cut the celebration short, but, since we have the next couple of days off, I've got a favor to ask." The others stopped their joking and drinking long enough to listen in. "Well, Audrey's the one making the request, but—"

"What does the counselor need?" Sergeant Delgado asked. As moody as he'd been lately, he had a soft spot for Audrey Kline, the assistant district attorney who'd put away the murderer of a little boy who'd died in Delgado's arms back in November. They all owed Audrey a favor for that conviction.

"She's looking for some extra security to keep an eye on the guests at Richard Eames's funeral tomorrow. I guess he'd been with the Mayweather family so long that they're all attending the service and hosting a reception afterward at the estate."

"They're *all* attending?" Trip was still pondering what accusations, or unlikely compliments, Charlotte had to say about him. She'd made it clear that she had a phobia about people, about strangers—about big, scary men like him, especially. He couldn't see her standing with a crowd of mourners around a grave site, or welcoming them into her home.

"Charlotte said Richard Eames was like an uncle to her. They're going to find a way to sneak her in to the graveside service," Alex explained. "But they're worried about paparazzi and curious fans. Anything about the Mayweathers is usually newsworthy, but if word gets out that Charlotte is finally making a public appearance after all these years, it might bring the crazies out. They'd like to keep their mourning as private as possible, of course."

"They're about the wealthiest family in Kansas City," Randy pointed out. "Don't they have their own security?"

Alex nodded. "Gallagher Security Systems—the

same private outfit that protects the estate where Audrey's father lives. They'll provide extra guards at the house, in addition to all the electronics Gallagher designed. But they're more gadgets than manpower—they don't have the resources to secure a cemetery the size of Mt. Washington as well."

Rafe Delgado leaned back in his seat, a frown settling back on his expression. "Didn't Gallagher provide the security at the estate where Gretchen Cosgrove was murdered, too?"

Randy picked up on his suspicion. "That's not a very good recommendation for Gallagher's company."

"Gallagher's wife was the Rich Girl Killer's first victim," Captain Cutler reminded them.

"If his company had access to all the crime scenes, maybe the second murder and other attempts are a cover for his wife's death." Randy wasn't getting the hint stamped on Cutler's unsmiling face. "Has anyone investigated him?"

The captain cleared his throat and simply looked at her.

Randy wilted in her chair. "Too soon in our relationship to speculate about something like that, hmm?"

"Quinn Gallagher is a friend of mine," Cutler explained. "Any connection between his company and the murders is a cruel coincidence. Or a plot to discredit him."

Trip's gaze instinctively shifted across the room to the table where Spencer Montgomery and his partner were sipping drinks. Son of a gun. The red-haired detective was looking over the rim of his glass, meeting Trip's gaze—as if he knew the conversation around SWAT Team One's table centered on his investigation.

The detective didn't so much as blink before turning back to his partner. A guy that unflappable would have no qualms about exploiting Charlotte Mayweather's grief if it meant solving his case.

Uh-uh. He had the stitches in his arm to prove *he* was the man Charlotte could count on if there was any other threat to her person or sanity—from killer or cop alike. Whether she believed it or not.

Trip pulled back to answer Alex. "I'll volunteer."

The mood around the table grew sober. They were all shifting back into wary-protector mode.

"Jackson Mayweather is looking for some off-duty officers to help with crowd control, in exchange for a generous donation to KCPD's widows and orphans fund."

"Whatever the Mayweathers need. I'm there."

"Thanks, Trip."

Captain Cutler was nodding, pushing away from the table and standing. "Call or text us with the times and setup. We can coordinate our efforts once we're on-site. And remember, protecting the Mayweathers is strictly voluntary."

"I'll be there," Trip repeated, rising.

Alex stood, too. "Audrey will be there all day, so that means I will, too."

Randy shrugged and joined in. "It's not like I've got a hot date tomorrow."

Rafe was looking over his shoulder, watching Josie serve a beer and a smile up to one customer before hurrying behind the counter to greet someone new and fetch the next drink. Whatever was troubling him didn't appear to be a concern for her.

"Sarge?" the captain prompted.

Rafe stood as well. "I'm in."

Trip grabbed his jacket off the back of his chair and shrugged into it. With thoughts of Charlotte distracting him from his normal routine, he hadn't really been in the mood to celebrate, anyway. As the others headed for the door, he picked up his book and fell into step behind them. Any mental thumbing of the nose as they filed past Spencer Montgomery's table was a silent bonus.

This was a team he could trust. Just like that drill this afternoon—they'd get the job done. Together.

Sure, maybe he was looking to redeem himself in Charlotte's eyes. Maybe he couldn't make her feel safe, or put the woman at ease, but he damn sure could handle a little routine security and crowd control. He could ensure that she found the privacy she needed to deal with her grief.

And maybe that knowledge, at last, would put his guilty conscience to rest.

Chapter Five

Charlotte's palm was sweaty around the wrapped bouquet of white roses she'd been clinging to for the past twenty minutes.

While Max chewed on his new leash at her feet, she sat at the tinted back window of her father's limo, secretly watching the mourners huddled around a green tent some fifty yards from where the driver had parked near the beginning of the procession line. Her head ached with a terrible mix of guilt and grief. The sweeping hillside, studded with tall trees and marble markers, was curtained by rain and shadows, giving a twilight cast to the afternoon service.

The event-planning team her father had hired to put together a reception at the house later was to be commended for stepping in to help with the ceremony here, as well. Not only had they taken over the task of coordinating transportation from Mt. Washington Cemetery to the estate, they'd issued umbrellas to any guest who'd shown up for the wet proceedings without one.

Like a sea of black mushrooms sprouting across the hillside, the faceless mourners only added to Charlotte's unsettled nerves. Logically, she understood there were people here she knew and could trust. But she couldn't see any of them. Her father and stepmother would be standing beneath the awning with the family and minister. Audrey and Alex were there, too. She'd seen him drive up in his black SWAT uniform earlier, no doubt taking a break from work to attend the service with his fiancée. But without the anchor of a trusted friend or family member to cling to, an illogical sense of isolation was creeping in, making Charlotte question the impulse to pay her personal respects to an old friend.

A flicker of movement at the edge of the crowd caught her attention and she shifted in her seat. Her stepbrother, Kyle Austin, turned away from the ceremony to check his watch. The shoulders of his tailored gray suit lifted with a deep breath and another check of the time before he disappeared beneath his umbrella again. While she'd grown up with Richard Eames, the Austins had been part of the family for less than two years, and Kyle was such a workaholic at her father's real estate development company that he barely knew the staff's name. He was here strictly as a courtesy to her father.

Drawn to another ripple of movement, she spotted her stepsister Bailey's strawberry blond hair. She was standing with her arm linked to a tall blond man. Charlotte squinted. If he bent down from beneath that umbrella and whispered to Bailey just one more time…Harper Pierce? Charlotte smiled as he kissed her stepsister's cheek, recognizing the society prince she'd once gone to school with.

In the very next breath, she frowned. Harper had proposed to their classmate Gretchen Cosgrove last year. According to her best friend Audrey, within a month after Gretch was murdered, he'd made a play for her. Audrey, of course, an eloquent woman who rarely minced words, told him in no uncertain terms that Alex Taylor was the man she loved and Harper needed to move on.

Now he was spending time with Bailey? They knew each other well enough to hold hands and exchange a kiss? When had that happened? Gretchen had been dead for only four months. A man that desperate for constant female companionship seemed a far cry from the high-school soccer hero she'd once had a major crush on. When she was sixteen, even though he'd never looked at her as anything other than his study buddy, she'd willingly typed Harper's papers and tutored him in whatever subject he struggled with in order to maintain the academic standards needed to play sports at Sterling Academy.

The notion of high school and longing for a boy of her own turned her memories to the stupid choice she'd made with one of Harper's teammates the night of the prom. It was a plain girl's foolish mistake to turn down attending with a friend and accept Landon Turner's invitation. Finding out he'd issued the invitation on a lousy hundred-dollar dare, and had another girl waiting for him at the dance, had led to a humiliating exit. And to the man waiting in the parking lot. And the speeding van and the…

"Nope." Charlotte turned away from the window, thinking she could turn away from the memories, as well. "I'm not reliving that nightmare again."

And yet she was. Right now. Hiding away in a car because she was so damn afraid of some other stranger out there. How was she any less free of her kidnappers now than when they'd held her down and cut off part of her ear as proof of life for her father?

Landon had paid for his unwitting collusion with the kidnappers by being kicked out of Sterling Academy and losing his most prestigious scholarship offers. Once he'd outgrown the need to play pranks on the school's resident bookworm, he probably had gone on to lead a normal, successful life.

But she was still paying for that night. She was still afraid, still obeying the threat that her kidnappers would find her and hurt her even worse, in any number of ways, if she tried to escape and trust her own decisions and be free again.

With a weighty, sorrowful sigh, she pulled her

black trench coat more tightly around the skirt and sweater she wore. She let her fingers slide into her pocket to touch the brand-new phone with the unlisted number that her father had given her. She could call for help anytime she needed to. Too bad there wasn't a number she could call to make her feel truly warm and confident and normal again.

When the low tones of "Amazing Grace" filtered in through the walls of the limo, Charlotte turned her attention toward the green tent again. The service was winding down and people were moving, probably to lay a flower on the casket or express condolences to Mrs. Eames, her children and grandchildren. Charlotte's heart rate picked up a notch in anticipation. She wanted to be one of those people trading hugs, holding someone close to share her grief.

But she couldn't. Even if she could see some faces now, they were all strangers to her. How could she face them, wondering if the man who'd killed Richard and terrorized her was one of them? Was there someone else in that crowd waiting to knock her senseless and take her away from everything she knew and loved in exchange for her father's money? Was there someone out there who wanted to kill her, too?

Besides, the mourners weren't the only crowd at Mt. Washington today. Down at the bottom of the hill, at a restricted distance beyond the line of cars, was a gathering of reporters, complete with microphones and television cameras. They might be waiting for a glimpse of Jackson Mayweather or a sound bite from one of his stepchildren or second wife, but there'd be a crazy dash if they knew that, after ten years of hiding from Kansas City society, the Mad Miss Mayweather had ventured out of her ivory tower. And no matter how badly she wanted to pay her respects, she wouldn't risk the potential media circus of her appearance detracting from the Eames family and the sadness of the day.

So she'd sit right where she was until the crowd cleared and her father came to get her to walk her up to the grave site.

When she realized she was watching the clock as closely as her time-obsessed stepbrother, Charlotte flipped her watch around on her wrist and reached down to scratch Max's head. "We just need to be patient. After ten years of solitude, you'd think I'd know how to do that, right?"

Max answered with a sniff of her hand and a bored look in his round brown eyes. Leaving him to polish off his chew toy, she returned to the task of spying from her anonymous vantage point. The mourners were spread out across the hillside now, trickling down to their cars—walking in small groups, stopping to chat with old friends. As the crowd thinned, she spotted Alex and Audrey with one of the uniformed guards from Gallagher Security. Two motorcycle cops from KCPD cruised by, pulling into position at the front of the procession.

A tall man climbed out of a police SUV parked up ahead, hunching his shoulders against the rain as he crossed the road to speak to the traffic cops. Charlotte pulled one knee beneath her and sat up taller. She recognized that man in the black SWAT uniform. Salt-and-pepper hair. Air of authority. He was Alex's captain, one of the men she'd seen him talking to the night of Richard's murder.

A second man from Alex's team, lanky, with dark brown hair beneath his black SWAT cap, climbed out from the passenger side of the SUV. He lowered the walkie-talkie he'd been speaking into and pointed up the hill.

Spinning in her seat, Charlotte followed the direction of his arm. She searched higher up the hill, beyond the green tent, and saw the policewoman with the blond ponytail looking through a pair of binoculars.

Charlotte searched the entire crowd, from one tree line to the next. If the rest of Alex's team was here, did that mean…?

Trip Jones.

Her pulse skipped a beat then drummed into overtime. How had she missed seeing the oversize mountain of a man in the black uniform and boots standing near the media cars and trucks, squinting into the drizzling rain because he had no hat?

The water added nutmeg-colored streaks to his light brown hair. The rain had to be running down the back of his neck, making his crisp uniform damp and sticky. One hand rested on the butt of the gun strapped to his thigh, the other tapped at the tiny microphone clipped to his ear as his lips moved in some sort of terse reply. But she detected no hint of discomfort in his implacable stance, no trace of complaint in the methodical back-and-forth scan of his eyes.

"Maximus, I think we owe the guy a new hat." And an apology. And maybe an explanation for her odd behavior.

And maybe while she was doing that, she could study those hazel eyes again, to see if she'd only imagined the gentle humor and unflinching support there when he'd handed her Max and told the others at that ambulance to bug off.

Of course, to do that, she'd have to meet him again. She'd have to be close enough to make that eye contact. She'd have to speak. Rationally. But she hadn't seen any pigs flying around—

A sharp knock on the window beside her made her jump halfway across the seat. Max's woof matched her startled gasp. Clutching her hand over her thumping heart, Charlotte reminded herself to breathe and called herself twenty kinds of fool once she identified the man with the wire-rimmed glasses waiting patiently outside the car.

Jeffrey Beecher was the executive assistant for the event company handling the memorial reception today. The earbud he wore and corkscrew cord that curled down beneath his suit jacket confirmed that he was the hired help. Her stepmother often employed Jeffrey and his crew to coordinate parties and fundraisers. Charlotte didn't attend those functions, but her father ran thorough background checks and made sure that she was introduced to any staff who came onto the estate. Just in case she would need to leave her rooms during an event, she would be able to identify the employee and not go into a panic.

She briefly considered staying where she was and not responding to the knock. But Max had barked and she had yelped, and the man with the business suit and umbrella really was standing ever so patiently in the rain, so he had to know she was in here.

Just do it, Charlotte. She had no place to withdraw to right now. *Engage.*

Crawling back across the leather seat, Charlotte pushed the button and lowered the window a few inches—just enough to peek through and smell the green, woodsy dampness in the cool outside air. "Yes?"

Jeffrey's umbrella blocked the rain as he bent over far enough to line his eyes up with hers. He adjusted his glasses on his nose and smiled. "Miss Mayweather. Sorry to intrude on your privacy. But

I need to tell you there's been a slight change in plans."

"Oh?" She didn't like change. She didn't like surprises.

Something of her confusion must have read on her face, because he put up a hand and patted the air in a placating gesture. "Don't worry. We'll still get you up to lay a flower on the grave and say your goodbyes. But I'll have to ask you to wait in the car a little bit longer."

She reached down to stroke Max's ears. "Is something wrong?"

He quickly shook his head to reassure her. "We weren't anticipating the numbers of reporters here at the cemetery, so we're having to improvise. Clarice," his boss, "actually invited them to attend the reception. As long as they stay outside of the gates, of course."

Charlotte climbed up onto her knees again, her gaze flitting over to the news vans and photographers and the mountain of a man keeping watch over them. Would they really try to intrude on the family's privacy with Trip standing guard?

Her father apparently thought so. "Mr. Mayweather is going to send your stepmother and stepsister on to the house so that the press corps will follow them. Then he'll come back for you to lay the flowers on the grave."

"What about Kyle?"

"Oh, yes." His gaze darted over to Kyle Austin, jogging down the hill. Charlotte saw her blond-haired stepbrother collapse his umbrella, climb into his white Jaguar and speed away from the service. She had no time to speculate where he was going in such a hurry because Jeffrey was pulling an envelope from inside his jacket and sliding it through the crack in the window. "Kyle said a man handed this to him, but he needed to get back to the office, so he asked me to deliver it to you."

Charlotte plucked the envelope from his fingers. "What man?"

"He didn't know him, but he said he had on a uniform of some kind. Your name is on the envelope." Jeffrey shrugged. "I'm assuming it's a condolence?"

She turned it over to see her name neatly typed on the front. But there was no return address, no glimpse of handwriting to give her any clue as to who it might be from. Maybe this was Trip Jones's idea of sending her an apology?

Only, *he* wasn't the one who needed to apologize.

She pulled the envelope into her lap and tried to be civil. "Thank you, Jeffrey."

"No problem." Something buzzed into the earbud he wore and he answered with a "yes, ma'am" before pulling away. "Sorry to intrude on your privacy, Miss Mayweather, but I'd better get to the estate and make sure everyone's ready when the guests arrive. See you there."

Probably not. Charlotte rolled the window up and sat back to open the envelope and pull out the neatly folded letter inside, alternately checking out one window and then the other for any sign of her mysterious pen pal. So a man in uniform had given it to Kyle. One of the security guards? Someone on the florists' staff? A courier? Police officer? Trip?

Or someone very different.

It's your turn, Charlotte.
All those brains, yet you never saw me coming.
I'm here now. Watching. Waiting.
The old man couldn't stop me from getting to you. No one can. I'll take what you owe me and enjoy watching you squirm.
Scared yet?

"Oh, God." The silent assault pushed the blood to her feet, making her feel dizzy, light-headed. Her vision blurred the vile words as she crumpled the letter in her fist. "Max?" She instinctively reached for the dog. "Max?"

He hopped onto the seat beside her and she hugged him tight. But she still felt cold, isolated, afraid.

"Why is this happening to me?" she whispered

into the dog's fur, rocking back and forth. "Why does he want to hurt—?"

The phone in her coat pocket rang and she screamed out loud. Max barked but licked her hand as her shaking fingers dug into the pocket of her coat.

It rang again, the chirping sound creeping along her skin and raising goose bumps. It was him. She knew it was him and she answered anyway. "What?"

A single, satisfied breath. And then, "Did you get my message?"

"Stop this." Anger and confusion colored her plea. "I'm not like other people. I can't handle this."

Another soft breath ended in a low-pitched laugh. "Don't you think I know that?"

Charlotte slapped the phone shut and hurled it across the limo.

It started ringing again as soon as it settled into a carpeted corner of the floor. "Stop it!"

She snatched Max's leash and shoved the car door open. Her feet slipped on the red bricks that lined the road, and she grabbed onto the door handle to keep from falling. One shoe came off and tumbled into the ditch. She didn't care that her stockings were soaking up the oily residue on the asphalt. She had only one thought in mind as she spun around to search the hillside. "Dad?"

Her gaze darted from umbrella to umbrella, from

marker to marker. She needed the cool rain splashing her face to clear her senses enough to realize that she'd just captured the attention of half the people milling through Mt. Washington.

For an instant, Charlotte froze. Her skin heated with embarrassment, her thoughts raced with panic. The man who'd called her was here. Watching. Taking delight in her phobic reaction to his threats.

Stay in the moment, Charlotte. Don't let him make you crazy.

What a fool she was. *Just go home. Don't give him the satisfaction of seeing you like this.*

Using her hand more than her vision to guide her, she tugged Max's leash and sidled around the front of the car. She knocked on the driver's window, peered inside behind the wheel. Empty. Where had he gone? This wasn't part of the plan.

"Did you need me, Miss?"

The smell of smoke filled her nose as she twirled around. "My father gave you specific instructions to wait…"

Uniform.

"I was just taking a cigarette break, ma'am. Union allows it. I was right over there."

She read the name on his chest beneath the event company's logo. *Bud.*

She didn't know any Bud.

"Did you…?" She raised the crumpled note in her hand. "Did you give this to my brother?"

"Ma'am?" Bud tucked a toothpick into the corner of his mouth and frowned. "Is something wrong?"

"Charlotte Mayweather!"

She turned to the sound of the voice. Snap. A bright light flashed in her eyes and she jerked her face away.

"Hey, pal." Bud in the uniform stepped between her and the photographer who was trying to snap another picture. "You leave her alone."

Move.

The photographer with the receding hairline wasn't the only reporter calling her name. While he traded curses with Bud, Charlotte blinked her eyes clear and looked over the hood of the limo, seeking out a familiar face. Any familiar face.

Red hair. "Audrey?"

The moment she spotted her friend hurrying down the hill with Alex Taylor at her side, Charlotte limped around the car on one shoe. With a click of her tongue to command him, Max leaped over the ditch with her and scrambled up the hill.

Another light flashed in her peripheral vision and she turned up the collar of her trench coat, pulling her head in like a turtle and skirting past a black-marble marker to reach her friends.

"Charlotte, what's happened?" Audrey wrapped

her up in a hug and Alex's strong arms folded around them both.

"He called me on my new phone. He's here."

Alex urged them both down the hill toward the cars, his chin tipped toward the microphone on his collar. "Come to my location now," she heard, as he guided them across the ditch. "And get those photographers back. Lassen, you son of a..." Alex pulled back and pressed a kiss to Audrey's temple. "Get her in the car while I take care of this rat."

With Audrey's arm around her shoulders, they turned toward the limo. "Steve Lassen is that tabloid opportunist who gave me such grief during my gang-leader trial last November. He and Alex have history."

Charlotte saw Bud circling around the limo, opening the back door for them. She planted her feet, tripping out of her second shoe before they stopped. "I don't want to go with him."

"Char, the press..." She pulled the letter from Charlotte's hand. Audrey's pale cheeks flooded with color. "Where did you get this?"

Men in black uniforms were closing in on their position near the hood of the limousine. Orders were shouted, protests made. But the press was retreating to the opposite side of the road.

"Oh, my God." Charlotte willingly turned her back to the cameras and squeezed Audrey's hand, worried by her friend's reaction to the threat. "This is just like the one I got last November. Alex!"

"Jeffrey—the guy organizing all this—said it was from Kyle, that a man in some kind of uniform had given it to him."

Alex was back. He wound his arm around Audrey and read the note.

"Where's Jeffrey now?" Audrey asked, futilely trying to look beyond Alex's protective grasp.

"Leave that to the detectives. He's back," Alex announced grimly.

"Who's back?" Charlotte whispered, more alarmed by the way Audrey's cheeks blanched than by anything that had happened in the past few minutes.

"The Rich Girl Killer."

It was a bleak, terrifying pronouncement.

"The man who killed Gretchen and Val?" The man who'd worked with a gang to terrorize Audrey? He was after *her?*

"Here," Alex ordered, thrusting out the letter. Charlotte shivered from head to toe at the wall of black looming up behind her. She recognized the hand that reached around her to take the paper from Alex and shrank away from the fading bruise of a dog nip there. "Get that letter out of the rain—it could be evidence. I need to get Aud someplace safe."

"We'll get the family home." Captain Cutler was

there, too, snapping orders. "Jones, get this one back to the limo and tell that guy to drive."

"Sorry, I've got to do this." Trip's deep voice seemed to hold a real apology as he stuffed the letter inside his vest and pulled Max's leash from her fingers. But there was nothing forgiving about his big hand clamping around her arm, pulling her into step beside him. "But the closer you are to me, the safer you'll be."

"Let me go." Charlotte struggled every step of the way. But her wet feet found no traction and Trip's grasp on her arm showed no signs of freeing her.

"Get in the car," Trip ordered.

Her eyes zeroed in on Bud, rolling his toothpick from one side of his mouth to the other as he waited for her.

"No." She didn't know Bud, couldn't ride with him. "No!" When she realized she couldn't stop the freight train of Trip's long strides, she reached up and grabbed a handful of his sleeve. Her fingers curled into the damp material, wrinkling it in her fist. "I don't trust him. He's wearing a uniform."

Trip planted his feet and faced her, his hand on her arm the only thing keeping her from pitching forward at the sudden stop. "*I'm* wearing a uniform."

There was no humor in the green-gold gaze bearing down on her now.

Her fingertips brushed against the muscle flexing beneath his sleeve, their pleading grasp stuttering at the unfamiliar sensations of hardness and heat. She snatched her fingers away, fighting the unexpected urge to hold on tighter, wiping the moisture from her glasses instead. "A man in uniform handed the letter to Kyle, who gave it to Jeffrey, who gave it to me. But I was watching you when I received it, so I'm guessing you didn't—"

"You make no sense. Back up!" She flinched as he pointed over her head toward a reporter inching across the road. She flinched again when his hand settled on her shoulder. With a sotto-voce curse, he moved it away. He bent his knees, hunching down to bring his gaze more even with hers. "Why did you get out of the car in the first place? The plan was to take you up to the site after the procession had left."

"But he said the plans had changed—"

"Who said? The driver?" He swung his gaze toward Bud, patting his chest where the letter was hidden. "You think *he* sent this?"

"He's wearing a uniform."

"Miss Mayweather?" a voice shouted from the other side of the road. "Does today's visit mean you're coming out of seclusion?"

"That's Jackson's daughter?"

"How does she look?"

Charlotte's world shrank to the wall of black Kevlar in front of her face as Trip straightened and shouted a second warning to the reporters clamoring for the scoop of the day. She couldn't tell if he was moving or if she was the one drifting closer when the cameras started flashing.

"Is your driver's murder part of another threat against your family?" one reporter asked.

"Oh, my God." It was definitely her who had taken that step away from the limelight. "I don't want the Eames family to hear any of this today. It was a mistake to come."

"Miss Mayweather—hurry." Bud was waving her toward the limo's open door.

"This is crazy." Trip grumbled his frustration and released her to pick up Max and drop all twenty-five pounds of him into her arms. Instead of pushing her toward the car, he tucked her to his side and hustled her in the opposite direction, half lifting her so that her toes touched the bricks and asphalt only every third step or so. "I guess you two are stuck with me."

"Stop. Where are you taking me? Put me down."

"I'm obeying an order."

Too close. Too fast. She couldn't breathe. She needed to think. Charlotte squiggled her hips and pushed with her elbow. If she let Max go, maybe she could free herself. But if she let go, there'd be nothing between her and Trip Jones. "You're not listening to me."

"You can have Bud or those reporters or me."

Somewhere between the sensations of chilled toes and warm man, she'd missed seeing just how far he'd taken her. Her feet scraped the ground as he wedged her back against the side of a heavy-duty black pickup truck. Max was squirming, woofing under his breath at the flashes of light that warned the reporters were pursuing them, but Trip put an arm beneath hers to keep the dog in place as he pulled out a set of keys. The lock beeped and he had the door open before she pulled away from his helping hand and her fear found its voice. "I feel like I'm being kidnapped again."

"What?" He retreated half a step, his eyes narrowing, perhaps judging her sincerity, perhaps deeming her a lunatic. "If you want to be safe, get in. Hell, I'll give you the damn keys and you can drive if you'll just move."

"I don't have a license anymore. I can't drive. I'm afraid we're at a standoff." Instead of voicing the argument that rounded his lips, he put his hands on her waist and lifted her and Max into the truck. "Hey!"

After tossing aside a paperback novel that had been sitting on the seat, he reached across her and fastened the seat belt around her. "Now get down before those cameras or someone else gets a clean shot at you."

He gave her a split second to pull Max out of the way before he closed the door and jogged around the truck to climb in behind the wheel. Charlotte's fingers toyed with the handle then hesitantly reached down to pull the paperback from the floorboard. She ran her fingers over one of her favorite titles as she folded it shut. "You bent your book cover."

Trip reached across the center console and snatched the book from her hands, tossing it onto the folding seat behind him. "It's been a long time since anyone made me think I was some kind of stupid bully."

Feeling trapped but a fraction more secure in here than she did on the other side of the door, she huddled against it, slinking down behind Max while Trip started the engine. "I never said you were stupid."

"Nice distinction." Trip scrubbed his hand over his face, taking the rain and his frustration with it, before turning to look at her across the seat. His deep voice rumbled inside the cab of the truck. "You're my only concern, Charlotte. What I say to you will always be the truth. I've got your back. I won't hurt you. And I won't let you get hurt."

"You can't promise something like that." She pulled off her fogged-up glasses and squinted to keep him in focus. "I know I'm a bit of…" an odd duck? a crazy lady? "a paranoid freak—"

"You're not."

"—but I have reason to be. It's hard for me to trust anyone besides Dad…or Richard." Her eyes lost focus as the grief and injustice of the day took hold again.

Trip put the truck into gear, honked to clear the road and pulled out. "Honey, I don't need you to walk and talk like every other woman on the planet. I just need you to believe that I'm one of the good guys. Have a little faith."

Hearing a grown man call her *honey* diverted Charlotte's thoughts long enough to lose her grip on Max. The traitorous dog had no confusion whatsoever about Trip Jones. He walked right over to Trip's lap and sniffed his face.

With a muttered reprimand and a tussle around the ears, Trip pushed him away. "Your dog likes me. Why can't you?" He braked the truck before taking a hairpin turn toward the cemetery's main gate. "Now hold on."

As they picked up speed, Trip called his captain on his ear mike, giving something called a "twenty" and promising an ETA as soon as he confirmed a destination.

Like him? So she was a little fascinated with his taste in reading and the way he handled her dog and why on earth he'd call her *honey*. And she was more curious than she should be at the self-deprecation she'd heard in his "stupid bully" line.

But trust him?

Charlotte kept her eye on Trip's stiff expression, held tight to Max and prayed.

Chapter Six

The craziness they'd left behind at the cemetery was waiting for her at home, too.

A team of Gallagher Security guards was sorting out the traffic jam at the front entrance to the Mayweather estate, asking for IDs and punching in security codes to allow expected guests through the gates, while filtering out any paparazzi or curiosity seekers posing as mourners and trying to sneak in. Jeffrey Beecher, wearing a clear plastic raincoat over his suit and tie, carried a clipboard and his cell phone. He greeted each vehicle, checked his guest list and either signaled to the guards to let the people inside pass, or got on the phone to verify whether someone should be allowed to enter.

Charlotte was still hunkered down in the passenger seat of Trip's truck, absently stroking Max's fur, barely peeping through the bottom of the window. They were seven vehicles back, with more cars and limousines pulling into the queue behind them. A television news crew had a camera and antenna set up on top of its van across the street, and another was filming a live feed with its reporter on the street. Trip was on his phone, calling in a situation report, telling his captain that she was fine but that he was going to need backup on the scene if they had any hopes of securing it. Not an encouraging thought.

There were whistles and bright lights, shouts and honking horns. The strident echo of sirens pierced the thick air, probably in answer to neighborhood complaints about the streets being blocked. The windshield wipers beat at a steady cadence and her heart thumped in the same quick rhythm. Her feet hurt. And every time she tried to inhale a calming breath, her nose filled with the pungent scent of wet dog fur and something even more unsettling that had taken her ten miles of riding in the truck to identify—the earthy scent of wet, warm, male skin.

"This is my own home," Charlotte murmured, wilting at the assault on her senses. "My sanctuary."

She needed quiet, alone and safe right now. But there was nothing outside the truck or inside her own head that could generate any sense of calm.

"Yeah, it's a real zoo here." Even as he continued to speak on the phone, Trip's right hand moved across the center console.

Was he reaching for her? Offering comfort? For one disjointed moment, Charlotte pulled her fingers from Max and let them drift across the seat toward the long, bruised fingers.

"You okay?" he mouthed the words and Charlotte looked into those unflinching eyes and almost nodded.

But just as she imagined she could feel the heat emanating from Trip's big hand, the screech of tires on the wet pavement drew her attention back outside. The crunch of metal on metal grated against her ears as she sat up in time to see one of the cars ahead of them plow into the rear bumper of another.

"Son of a gun." Trip sat up straighter, too, his taut posture instantly putting her on guard. "Gotta go, sir. Fender bender. Could be the tension of the day, could be a diversion. I'll keep you posted." The captain said something else and Trip glanced over at Charlotte. "Like glue. Jones out."

Trip's promise to Captain Cutler as he disconnected the call should have reassured her. But now people were out of their cars, inspecting the damage. One of the guards hurried over to assess the situation.

"You think the wreck was deliberate?" Charlotte asked, hating the possibilities.

Trip checked his rear- and side-view mirrors, his suspicions fueling Charlotte's own. "Half of Gallagher's men are leaving their posts, and there's no way a traffic cop could get in here fast. We're stuck."

"So what do we do?"

"Stay put." But Trip ignored his own edict and unfastened his seat belt. "Ah, hell."

Charlotte curled her fingers around Max's collar when Trip leaned forward. "What is it?"

"Are you sure that guy's working *for* you?"

She followed his gaze to see Jeffrey Beecher pointing to her in the truck and saying something to the guards. He might as well have shot up a flare because a pair of guards was now heading toward the truck. Even though Jeffrey's gestures indicated that he wanted to get Charlotte inside the gate as quickly as possible, car doors were opening, windows were going down and the line of cameras parked across the street swiveled their way.

"It's happening again," Charlotte despaired, feeling the unwanted attention crawling across her skin. "Why do they care so much about me being here?"

"They don't care about you. They want to sell papers."

"My father has friends at the *Kansas City Journal* and local TV stations. Ever since the kidnapping, they've agreed not to publish pictures and stories about me. Why would they risk their relationship with Dad to get a couple of pictures?"

"Steve Lassen's a tabloid photographer. He's independent, like a lot of these bozos. I'm guessing your daddy's influence hasn't reached the rags he works for yet." Trip scanned from side to side, and she could almost see him checking off one observation after another. A wary energy pulsed around him, filling the truck, stirring Max to his feet and adding an edgy blend of excitement and trepidation to Charlotte's fragile nerves. "You're a national story. After ten years of being a mystery woman, you made a public appearance at your chauffeur's funeral. Sounds like a headline to me. I'm guessing, in their minds, Daddy's influence only covers the privacy of your own home."

"That's not very comforting."

"If you want a guy to say it'll be all right when things are this crazy, I'm not your man." A muscle tensed along his jaw as he tempered the snap of his voice. "I'm more inclined to do something about the problem."

"I don't need any false platitudes."

"Fine." He shifted in his seat to pull his badge from his belt and loop it onto a chain around his neck. "You want to lie low in here until the guards can get us in? Or do you want me to clear a path now and take you straight to the house?"

"You can clear a path?"

He grinned, as if whatever permission she'd just given pleased him. "Like I said, I've got your back. Watch me work." He hopped out and faced her in the opening between the door and the frame. "Lock the doors and stay in the truck."

A spray of rain blew in, splashing her face like a wake-up call before he shut the door. He didn't budge until Charlotte scooted Max aside and scrambled across the seat to lock the door. Then, after laying a hand against the window he was gone, holding up his badge, identifying himself as KCPD and shouting orders that made the guards jump and people hurry back inside their cars. With each long stride that carried him into the fray, Charlotte felt more and more isolated—a pariah on display in the middle of all the chaos.

Steadfastly ignoring all the curious eyes turned her way, she wrapped her fingers around the steering wheel and held on, keeping Trip in sight. People straightened when he approached, jumped when he spoke. The gates swung open and he ushered the first two cars through to the driveway. Then he climbed onto the hood of one of the wrecked cars, rocking it up and down to unlock the bumpers.

Trip really was clearing a path to the house. One man versus a hundred, and he was winning. Her lips trembled with the unfamiliar urge to smile, but they settled into a straight line instead. What was it like to have that kind of confidence about the world? Would she ever be able to reclaim the adventurous spirit she'd had as a child? Before the kidnapping? Before the phobias and therapy and seclusion transformed her into this shadow of the woman she'd once hoped to be? Would she ever reclaim even half the strength that Joseph Jones, Jr., commanded?

As her thoughts took her to a darker place, Charlotte tightened her fingers on the wheel, willing the vibrations of the engine to flow through her and keep her anchored in the here and now. To trust Trip's word. To believe he could accomplish what he promised and get her safely home.

The dented cars separated and Trip, along with three other men, pushed both up onto the curb. He waved the fifth car in the queue into the narrow opening they'd created and pointed to the car just in front of her.

And then she caught the flicker of movement in the rearview mirror.

A man carrying a backpack darted from one car to the next, ducking down and hiding as he moved between them. Charlotte's knuckles popped out as she tightened her grip on the steering wheel and shifted her attention to the side-view mirror. There he was again, poking up behind another car. Oh, no. Even the rain couldn't mask the distinct points of his receding hairline or the camera slung around his neck.

"Steve Lassen." Charlotte breathed the vile paparazzo's name, hunching down and peering over the dashboard at the same time. True, he was staying across the street, but he was creeping closer and closer. "Hurry, Trip."

Then, boom. A loud smack hit the back of the truck and Charlotte sat bolt upright. Max propped his front paws on the back of the seat and barked at the bed of the truck. Had *she* been rear-ended, too? Charlotte checked the mirror. Nothing but the line of vehicles and endless rain behind her.

"Hush, Max. Hush, boy." She petted his flank and pulled him back down to the passenger seat.

A second mini-jolt hit and Charlotte spun around at the pinging sound. Was someone throwing rocks?

A bright flash from the trees across the sidewalk momentarily blinded her. That creep Lassen had maneuvered himself into position and finally had his picture of her—sitting behind the wheel of Trip's truck, wild-eyed, confused, afraid. Trip was running toward her, shouting something—drawing his gun and waving at her to get down.

A third projectile struck the glass beside her and Charlotte jumped. Max barked and barked and barked as she watched the window splinter into a fist-sized web of cracks right before her eyes.

"Shots fired!" She heard Trip's deep voice shouting in the distance. "Get down! Everyone, get down!"

Run. Fight. Move.

A surge of adrenaline, tamped down by caution and futility for too many years, screamed through Charlotte's veins, demanding she take action. She'd fought the night she'd been kidnapped, fought until too many blows and the mind-numbing drugs had taken away her ability to scream or struggle or even think.

"Charlotte!"

When she saw another, smaller flash near Steve Lassen's hiding place, Charlotte's instinct to survive grabbed hold of that adrenaline. *Gun!* She stepped on the brake and shifted the truck into Drive. The shot hit the window, shattering the glass as she stomped on the accelerator.

Trip slapped the side of the truck and jumped out of the path as it lurched forward. Max tumbled to the floorboards as Charlotte scraped past the car in front of her. "Sorry," and clipped the next one. "Sorry!"

"Charlotte, stop! Let me in!"

She heard Trip's curse, loud and clear, but couldn't seem to lift her foot off the accelerator or turn her focus from the haven of her home waiting at the end of that driveway.

Perched on the edge of the seat to reach the pedals, she held on tight as she bounced over the curb and spun for endless seconds, churning grass into mud. Finally, she remembered at least one thing from driver's ed in high school, hit the brake and twisted the wheel. With Trip charging up in her rearview mirror, she found the traction she needed and roared through the gate.

Her skills were rusty, but her speed was certain.

Bypassing the parking attendants and cars and guests at the front of the house, she drove around to the service entrance in back and skidded to a stop.

"Sorry, Max. Sorry, sweetie." Dragging the excited dog from the floorboards, Charlotte climbed out of the truck and ran to the back door.

The world outside was too frightening for her, too dangerous. She needed to be home. She needed to be safe.

She punched in the lock's security code, swung the door open and ran straight through the mudroom and kitchen and carpeted foyer. Concerned shouts and worried glances fell on deaf ears and tunnel vision. Max loped beside her as she turned down the first-floor hallway to her private suite of rooms. Blinded by the panic attack, she had to pause for a moment to catch her breath and steady her fingers to type in the unlock code to her room.

M-A-X-I-M-U-S.

Click.

She was in. "Go, boy." She released Max's leash and forced herself to breathe.

No more bullets. No more strangers. No more spotlight.

Push the door shut. You're safe—

A black boot wedged itself in the opening, stopping the door with a jerk. A big, bruised hand snatched hold of the door and pushed it back open.

Charlotte was forced to retreat as Trip Jones filled

her doorway and marched into her sitting room. "What the hell were you thinking?"

She spun around, snatching up the first object she came to—a small bronze shield from the museum. She held it up in front of her as her hips butted against the back of the sofa. "What are you doing here? I'll call security. This is my home. Get out."

"Uh-uh, honey. You stay right with me this time." He easily pried the shield from her hands and tossed it onto the cushions behind her. "I don't care what kind of crazy you are—you look me in the eye and talk to me."

"Hey, that's Etruscan."

"I don't care if it's the Mona Lisa." In the time it took her to glance down and ensure the security of the artifact she was responsible for, Trip had her pinned against the back of the couch, with one fist on the fabric at each side of her. His thighs were like tree trunks pressing into hers, his hair was dark with rain, his uniform splattered with mud, and his chest rose and fell in a quick, deep rhythm while he dripped on her. He was too big, too furious, too much man to be in here. "I just tracked mud all through that nice reception in the front rooms to get to you. Now, I said I had your back. I told you to stay put."

"It's not your job to protect me." She shoved at the big white letters on the front of his uniform, but neither the Kevlar nor the man moved.

If anything, he was coming closer, leaning in, forcing her to tilt her head back, way back. "It's my job to protect everyone in this city, especially when my captain gives me an order. Get you home safely." His hazel eyes searched her face, looking for an understanding that wasn't easy to give. And then they crinkled with concern. "Cripes, Charlotte— some unknown perp was shooting at you, and your response is to run from help?"

"I couldn't stay out there any longer. I had to get inside."

"I had to let that shooter go so I could run after you. You want me to cite you for driving without a license, inflicting property damage or scaring the crap out of me?"

He was scared? Huh? Her fingers drifted beneath the hard edges of his vest, needing something to hold on to to stop their trembling. She felt the abundant warmth and rapid beat of his heart beneath her fingertips and realized she wasn't the only one shaking here. "I'll pay for any damages. I'll buy you a whole new truck. Where's my backpack? I can write you a check from my trust fund right now."

"Missing the point." With cooler air rushing in between them, he turned away, raking his fingers through his short hair, leaving a mess of shiny wet spikes in their wake. When he faced her again, he propped his hands on his hips, assuming a posture that she guessed was supposed to make him look less threatening. He failed. "Normally I'm an easygoing man. But you are pushing my buttons right and left, lady. How was I supposed to know whether you'd been hit or not?"

With Trip standing between her and her bedroom door now, Charlotte had nowhere to go unless she made a mad dash to the bathroom. He deserved better than another door slamming in his face. Besides, after sharing that much forced contact with his thickly muscled body, she wasn't sure her legs would carry her that far.

She hugged her arms around her middle, mentally trying to hold her ground. "I couldn't think. I saw the man in the woods with the gun. I mean, I didn't see his face, but I saw the flash and then the window shattered. I had to do something."

She held her breath as he closed the distance between them again, then released it on a shaky sigh when he reached out with a single finger to unwind a lock of hair that had twirled around the temple of her glasses. The gentleness of the gesture, the husky softness of his tone, were completely at odds with the drenched warrior who'd been pushing *her* buttons a moment earlier. "*Are* you hurt?" He reached into his pocket and held up a tiny metal ball in his palm. "Thank God he was just shooting BBs."

"BBs?"

"I picked this one up off the street. I'll call in my team to sweep the area as soon as they're done at

Mt. Washington—see if we can find any trace of the shooter." He looped the curl around his finger and rubbed it with his thumb. "He didn't get to you, did he? No cuts or bruises?"

Charlotte slowly shook her head, savoring his touch on her hair almost as if it was a caress against her skin. "If he wanted to kill me, why not use real bullets?"

"You tell me."

Her voice hushed to match his. "Someone wanted my attention."

"Someone wanted to scare you."

"He succeeded." But neither of them laughed at the joke. Instead, she leaned toward the warmth of his hand near her temple. But when his fingers tunneled a little deeper and brushed against her damaged earlobe, she jerked away. "Please don't."

"Sorry, I thought I was reading the okay signal."

"You were. I mean, what does that mean?"

His eyes narrowed a moment in confusion, but then he reached for that single tendril of hair again. "It means you're interested in seeing what up close and personal is like between us. But not too close."

She nodded. "Just don't touch my ear."

"Sensitive, hmm?"

More than he knew.

"Your hair's wild."

"It's out of control."

"It's so soft." He was inspecting the curl with an

almost scientific fascination. "Yet it's strong enough to hold on to me."

Was this…banter? Why wasn't he moving away? Why wasn't she pushing him away? She thought all the rain would leave her chilled, but with him so close, she felt…feverish.

"I really am sorry about the truck. And your hat. And the stitches in your arm." Wow. She was a freak. But he still had her hair curled around his finger, stroking it. It was a sensual, soothing gesture, an intimate one between a man and a woman. They'd argued and now they were making up. It felt so…

Normal.

Her whole body began to shake now. She so couldn't do this.

"Trip," she wanted to confess, "I'm not like any other woman you're likely to meet."

"I noticed." His hard face turned boyish with a sly half grin. "You sure know how to keep a man on his toes."

"That's not what I'm trying to do." She reached up to straighten her glasses and to tuck the curl, still warm from his touch, behind her ear and beyond his reach. "I wasn't always this way—with the phobias and panic attacks. But I guess it's who I am now. I appreciate you doing the favor for Audrey and Alex, and checking in on me. But we have security here. It's probably better if you go now, before I find some other way to ruin your—"

"Miss Mayweather?"

Charlotte clenched her toes into the carpet at the sharp rap at the open door behind Trip. She hadn't locked up. She hadn't barricaded herself in the way she needed to. And now she had a man in her room. Two men.

"Ma'am. Just wanted to return this."

Bud held his cap in one hand as he rolled a toothpick with his tongue from one side of his mouth to the other and held out a cell phone. Her new cell phone. How had she forgotten, for even one moment, that the outside world wanted to hurt her? *"Did you get my message?"* A strange man's laughter echoed in her memory and chilled her to the bone.

"That's not my phone," she lied.

"I found it in the back of the limo. Who else's would it be?"

"I don't want it. These are my private quarters. Please leave."

"You need to step back into the hall, my friend." Trip swept past her—in one stride, two.

Charlotte reached for his hand. He stopped.

She'd just dismissed him, just denied wanting to feel anything like a normal man-woman relationship with him. And now she was clinging to his hand.

For a split second, he seemed just as stunned by the impulsive contact as she was. But then, before she could tell herself to let go, he folded his strong fingers around hers and pulled her close behind him, shielding her from an unwanted visitor more effectively than the carved Etruscan bronze had.

Trip's deep voice took command of the room. "You've been dismissed," he paused to read the name on the gray uniform, "Bud."

"I'm just trying to do a nice thing here."

She buried her face between Trip's shoulder blades, clutching both hands around his. "He called me on that phone."

"Whoa, I didn't call anybody. I didn't use any of your minutes." Trip was pushing Bud out the door. "I'm just returning what I found."

"I don't want it. Take it away."

"You heard the lady. Wait." Trip pulled one of the black gloves off his belt. He understood the *he* Charlotte was talking about. "I'll take the phone. Now go."

As Trip wrapped up the cell and closed the door, she could hear Bud whining all the way down the hall. "Thanks for going out of your way, Bud. Just trying to do my job, ma'am. Lousy thanks."

Trip turned before the voice faded. "When did you get another call from the killer?"

"How did he get that number? It was a brand-new phone."

He squeezed her fingers. "Charlotte, when?"

"At the cemetery. Just after I got that note. He was laughing at me, at…rattling me. That's why I panicked."

Trip swore. "That means he was close enough to watch you. He's getting off on your distress. Who has that kind of access to you?"

"No one does." With a jerky shrug, Charlotte pulled her fingers away from the warmth and strength of Trip's hand. Trying to hug away the chill that shook her from inside and out, she stepped around him and turned the doorknob. "At least, no one does when I'm locked in here. You'd better go, too."

Every muscle inside Charlotte reached out to the comforting, abundant heat of Trip's body when he walked up behind her. But her mind wouldn't give in and move the way her body wanted her to.

"There's safety in numbers, Charlotte—not isolation. Whatever's happening isn't going to stop just because you lock that door."

"What's happening is that someone's trying to drive me crazy. The phone calls, the notes, the loud noises—they're all things that happened to me when I was kidnapped. I know what they all mean now—the taunting and the terror. If this guy knows everything that happened—if that's what is waiting for me..."

"Why would someone want to do that to you?"

"I don't know." Her shoulders sagged. "But I can't go through that again. I'm not strong like I used to be. I just can't do it. Security and predictability in my routine mean everything to me now. Trip?"

Damn, couldn't the man take a hint? Now he was wandering through her sitting room, peeking into her bedroom and bath. He looked at the artifacts set on nearly every table and desk, checked the books on her floor-to-ceiling shelves, studied pictures on the walls. Charlotte huddled at the door and watched him circle.

"You know, when I was growing up, a lot of people misjudged me because I was already about this big when I started high school. Plus, I wasn't…the best student on the planet. I didn't like it when people pointed it out to me." He stopped in front of her wall of books, stroking the spine of one leather volume and then pointing to one of her degrees she had hanging on the wall. "You must be pretty smart."

"You're not a stupid bully, Trip."

"I said that out loud, huh?" His self-deprecating smile tickled something deep inside her, waking a compassion she wouldn't have thought a man of Trip's skills and strength would need or want. His eyes sought hers, and dared to look beneath the surface, from clear across the room. "My point is, people can change. If we're not who we want to be, we have the power to do something about it. I have dyslexia. Don't get me wrong, I've outgrown some of it as I've matured, and retrained my brain on how to read things. But it takes me time, you know, to read books and take tests and fill out forms. I've got so much to catch up on that I'm never gonna know everything I want to."

Charlotte took a step into the room. "How is that like surviving a kidnapping and having every decision you make, every person you meet, colored by that nightmare?"

"I'm guessing you've never been called stupid."

Her heart ached for the young man he'd once been. She couldn't imagine absorbing such an insult, especially as an adolescent. But surely that was all behind him. He was a grown man now, exuding enough confidence to fill the room. "I imagine it's a struggle—something you should take pride in for overcoming. Clearly, you're an intelligent man or you wouldn't have the job you do. You wouldn't be able to break down doors with tables or rig up leashes from handcuffs."

"Thanks. But I didn't always see myself that way." Trip strolled back toward the door. "You want to change. You cared about your friend who died and wanted to be there to honor him. You love that mutt of yours to pieces. Your eyes—" he shook his head, as if in wonder "—say everything you think and feel." He waved his fingers in front of her face. "You're the one who took *my* hand."

He was standing right in front of her now. She answered to the letters emblazoned at the middle of his chest. "I was more afraid of Bud than I was of you. It doesn't mean I'm ready to be normal again, that

I'm ready to make myself a target for some sadistic stalker who seems to know exactly what scares me the most. How am I supposed to fight when I don't know who or why I'm fighting?"

"All I'm saying is, you can change if you want to. You can be stronger. I'll protect you all the way until you get there if you say the word. But it won't be easy. I discovered I didn't have all my demons licked when I met you in that museum the other night."

Charlotte tilted her head to find a curiously indulgent smile waiting for her. "What does that mean?"

"In some ways, every time I run into you, it's like high school all over again. You make me feel like I have to prove something, and I haven't had to prove anything to anyone for a long time."

"You don't have to prove anything."

"Yeah, I do. You still don't trust me."

Well, he'd certainly kept his word about one thing. He didn't lie. So they both had things they wanted to change. *Good luck with that.* "If we were in high school, I'd be the four-eyed brainiac in college-prep classes and you'd be the resident bad boy in shop or auto mechanics. Our paths would never cross."

Her smile faded along with his. But then something warm and mischievous colored his eyes. Before she could speculate on the change, he slid his finger and thumb beneath her chin and tipped it up another notch. He caught her startled gasp beneath his lips and pressed his mouth against hers. The kiss was tender, warm, brief.

He paused for a moment, his breath whispering against her skin. Then he tunneled his fingers into the curls at her nape, dipped his head and kissed her again. More firmly this time—a little less gentle, a little more possessive. He caught her bottom lip between both of his and drew his tongue along the curve, triggering a moist arrow of heat that made her fingers latch on to his biceps and her insides go liquid. Her lips pouted out, chasing his, foolishly wanting more, when he pulled away. Trip grinned. "Then I'm glad we're not in high school."

She didn't deserve that grin, wasn't sure she could even remember the last time a man had kissed her— didn't think a grown man as sexy and strong as Trip ever had. Charlotte's brain was spinning with questions, and she felt a little too flustered to speak coherently at the moment.

Fortunately, Trip Jones had no trouble with words or kisses or flaky plain Janes with a quirk for every day of the week. He scooted her to one side and opened the door. "Lock this behind me. And remember, you haven't seen the last of me yet. I've got your back."

She pushed the door shut after he stepped into the hallway, then scrambled the code on the keypad to lock it securely. She turned and leaned back against the door, drawing in a weary, thoughtful breath. Could she really conquer her phobias the way Trip had apparently conquered his reading disorder? Could she stand up to a killer who seemed to want to literally scare her to death? Could she ever be normal enough to act on this unexpected bond she was building with Trip?

I've got your back.

Charlotte knew that Trip believed that promise. But could she?

THE MAN RAN HIS FINGERS around the tiny circular dent on the tailgate of the black pickup truck, relying on the steady fall of rain to wash away any prints he might leave behind.

The shot wasn't terribly accurate if the prankster had been aiming for Charlotte. The scattershot approach was definitely too messy for his tastes. The randomness of firing into a crowd left entirely too much to chance.

He flipped up his collar and walked around the truck that was still steaming from the heat of the engine and counted one, two, at least three or four shots, judging by the shattered glass sitting in a puddle on the driver's seat. He'd wager the press had gotten some interesting pictures for the evening news, although he doubted if Charlotte would ever see them or the headlines surrounding the day's events. Jackson Mayweather and all his money would see to that.

So what was the advantage to his unknown and unwanted accomplice's attempt when his call and missive at the cemetery had already produced the desired results of tearing away at Charlotte Mayweather's fragile sense of security?

Straightening, he slowly turned 360 degrees, squinting into the rain as if the other man was still out there. Who the hell would shoot at her?

He had his plan carefully mapped out. One step at a time. Take away her safety net of familiar faces and staid routines. Make the phone calls, send the notes. Make her face everything she feared—loud noises, strangers, crowds, drugs, violence, isolation—everything that had been in the papers about her kidnapping. And then he'd add death to her story.

On his terms. In his own good time.

He buried his hands in his pockets and chuckled, the sound swallowed up by the storm. There *was* something extraordinarily delightful in watching Charlotte screaming like a crazy woman behind the wheel of a truck as she barreled through the gates of her own home.

Crazy was good. Crazy was justice.

But he wanted the satisfaction of showing Miss Brainiac that she was no better than him. Telling him no. Treating him like the hired help. Ignoring the gallantry she didn't deserve.

She was *his* to destroy.

No one else's.

Now to get out of the damn rain and get back to work.

Chapter Seven

Trip cradled the china cup that was far too delicate for his fingers in his open palm, and settled for smelling the coffee he'd been served this morning. A good ten years had passed since he'd been summoned like a rookie being called on the carpet for blowing an arrest. And his morning briefings had never taken place at a swanky, old-money estate where this dining room alone was as big as his entire apartment.

But Captain Cutler had okayed it—had encouraged Trip to answer Jackson Mayweather's invitation to breakfast, especially if the serial killer who'd targeted Alex Taylor's fiancée last year was now back in the picture and had set his sights on Charlotte. SWAT Team One had a personal connection to this case. The captain had told Trip that as long as there was a threat to someone the team cared about, then the team itself was at risk. If he had an in to keep tabs on the investigation, then use it. Let Alex hole up with Audrey on twenty-four-hour protection detail while Sergeant Delgado, Randy Murdock and Captain Cutler held down the fort at KCPD head-quarters. Trip was here amongst the businessmen and lawyers and Fourth Precinct detectives to rep-resent the interests of the team.

Besides, the scenery here was more interesting than any morning roll call meeting or team briefing. And he wasn't talking about the suits and ties seated around one end of the long dining room table.

Trip leaned against the oak frame beside a bank of windows and peeked through the sheers into a tiny square of lawn surrounded by a tall fence covered in ivy. It had no gate he could see and was only ac-cessible from an entrance in the back of the house itself. It was separate from the rest of the detailed landscaping on the grounds, nothing but grass and a small patio. And he guessed it served one purpose.

Max, an energetic, one-eared mix of shepherd and terrier, jumped into Charlotte's arms. The two went down on the slick wet grass and rolled, and she came up laughing.

For one surreal moment, he thought the rare glimpse of sunshine between storm fronts was playing tricks on his eyes. Charlotte Mayweather laughing, unguarded—her mouth open and her tof-fee-colored curls bouncing around her head—stirred something warm and appreciative in his blood. Made him think of that unexpected urge he'd had to kiss her yesterday—and the even stranger sense of territorial rightness that had flowed through his veins when she'd kissed him back.

Maybe some ancient magic had gotten inside him when she'd cut him with that old sword. Because there was something about all the crazy that was Charlotte Mayweather that kept getting under his skin.

Maybe it was the glimpses of the woman she was meant to be, like the one he saw now, surrounded by fresh air and her precious pooch, that intrigued him. She was wearing bright red rain boots and didn't seem to care a lick that she had mud and grass stains splashed on her bottom and the elbows of her red-and-gold-striped rugby shirt. Her jeans skimmed over her healthy curves nicely, and other than the funky earrings that glistened like gold Aztec sunbursts, she looked more like an outdoorsy kind of woman than a locked-up recluse—a woman better suited to running with Max in a dog park, traipsing through archaeological ruins or camping out in a tent with him, a campfire and one sleeping bag.

Time out, big guy. One sleeping bag? So when exactly did that idea pop into his head? The woman had forced him to get a tetanus shot, put his truck in the shop and wounded his pride. So why was his body humming with the idea of discovering what other hidden treasures Charlotte possessed?

He had to be honest with himself and admit that the team wasn't the only reason he'd agreed to come this morning. He still had something to prove to Charlotte, and he wasn't giving up on getting her to believe that he was one of the good guys until she stopped looking at him with those big gray eyes as though he was part of the nightmares that made her so afraid of the world beyond that fence.

Detective Montgomery set his cup in his saucer and expressed his frustration with Jackson Mayweather's version of cooperation. "I would have preferred to interview your daughter yesterday at the cemetery, or here after the shooting. Eighteen hours after the event, memories get sketchy, clues disappear and so do my suspects."

Jackson leaned back in his chair at the head of the table. "If you want to question Charlotte, you'll do it here, with my lawyer and me present, or not at all."

Trip tuned back in to the conversation, guessing for a moment that no one had bothered to tell Charlotte about this meeting of the minds that seemed fixated on using her to solve the Rich Girl Killer case. And then he decided that Charlotte was too observant a woman to miss the vehicles lined up in front of her home, and suspected she was out there throwing a tennis ball for Max and muddying up her clothes in an effort to hide from any possible contact with the men in this room.

Including him?

Now there was an irritating thought.

Jackson Mayweather's svelte blonde wife, Laura, signaled to the attendant waiting by the breakfast buffet to circle the table with the coffeepot again. "You keep talking about Charlotte. What are you doing about protecting my Bailey? She's a rich girl, too."

Jackson reached across the corner of the table and squeezed her hand. "Don't worry, darling, I've stepped up security here. I'm paying Quinn Gallagher's security company for a round-the-clock physical presence on the estate."

"That protects Charlotte—she's a homebody."

Trip shook off the attendant's offer to heat up his full cup of coffee. "She goes to work at the museum, doesn't she?"

"When it's closed." Laura Austin-Mayweather dismissed Trip's question as easily as she dismissed the servant. Her focus was on whatever her husband had to say. "What about when Bailey has a party to attend? Or is out on a date?"

Jackson patted her hand as he pulled away. "I'll assign one of the guards to follow her 24/7."

Trip crossed to the table and set his cup and saucer down. "Are you making the same arrangements for Charlotte?"

With a gesture to an empty chair, Jackson asked him to sit. "That's why I invited you to this meeting, son. You and I need to have a discussion."

"I'm listening." Trip rested one hand on the back

of a chair and the other near his badge on his utility belt, opting to stand. He didn't fault Mrs. Mayweather for worrying about her daughter's safety, but he had a feeling the psychological and physical attacks on Charlotte were specifically *for* Charlotte, and that no one else in this family was in any real danger. He had a feeling Jackson Mayweather sensed that as well, but was humoring his wife.

But Spencer Montgomery wasn't in the mood to humor anybody. He reached inside the pocket of his suit coat. "My job isn't security. It's solving these murders. I would think getting a serial killer off the streets would make everyone feel safer. Now if you and your lawyer will allow me to resume my interview? Even secondhand observations might be helpful." He set a clear plastic evidence bag holding the cell phone Trip had taken off Bud Preston on the table. "Can anyone here tell me how this phone got into Miss Mayweather's hands? From what I understand, *she* doesn't go shopping for such things."

Trip scanned the men and woman at the table right along with Detective Montgomery. Mrs. Mayweather looked to her husband, who looked to his stepson, Kyle, whose gaze fixed on the man with the glasses sitting across the table from him.

Jackson seemed displeased with the silence. "As soon as Charlotte told me she wanted to attend Richard's funeral service, I realized she'd need a new phone to keep in contact with me."

The brown-haired man with the wire-framed glasses dabbed his napkin against his lips and cleared his throat. Jeffrey Beecher was here representing the event staff that had worked on the estate and at the cemetery. "You hired our company to make sure everything ran smoothly yesterday. Maintaining communication between your family and our staff at Mt. Washington and here was key to a successful day. So I took the liberty of providing phones for each family member."

Detective Montgomery made the notation in his notebook. "Who had access to the numbers besides you?"

"The clerk at the phone company. Anyone with access to their database."

"I'm talking about anyone here at the house— before the funeral."

Jeffrey returned Kyle's pointed glare, apparently willing to share information, but not to take blame. "Mr. Austin told me to get five phones that he could hand out before everyone left for the cemetery. I set them on the credenza in the foyer, like you asked."

Jackson tossed his napkin on the table and faced his stepson. "Kyle, I asked you to get that new number for Charlotte—to help your sister. She trusts the family."

"I had things to do yesterday, Jackson. Meetings. The hired help was right there, willing to do what-ever we needed. I delegated."

Trip cared less about the family dynamics and more about the obvious lapse in security. "So the phones were sitting there all morning. Anyone in this house could have gotten the number and called her with the threat—family, regular staff, event staff, guests."

Jackson drummed his fist on the table. "You will not accuse my family of any wrongdoing. We're the victims here."

No, Charlotte and Richard Eames were the only victims in this house. "Sir, with all due respect, you asked me here this morning to report everything that happened while I was with your daughter. You wanted someone from the outside with no connection to your family to share his observations. You must have some suspicions."

"I asked you here because you're a SWAT cop, as finely trained as any elite military officer."

Kyle snickered into his coffee cup. "He called you because you're the only man with a gun and a badge that she's let close enough to do her any good these past ten years."

"Kyle," Laura chided her son.

He swallowed the last drop and set down his cup. "The last man she trusted enough to protect her outside this house was murdered. I can see why he'd rather have this Robocop than an old man around to look after her."

Trip's hand fisted around the top rung of the chair.

Thank goodness Charlotte wasn't here to hear that cold bit of compassion. "Well, then—speaking as a representative of Charlotte's best interests—her stalker is someone who's been in this house, right under your nose. Now I don't know if it's the same guy as the Rich Girl Killer, but I do know she's not safe here. It's an illusion you can't keep letting her live with."

"My daughter is very fragile."

"Thank you." Kyle threw up his hands as if he'd just scored a point. "I've been trying to tell you that Char's eccentricities border on mental instability."

"You're not helping, Kyle."

"I'm the one watching your money, Jackson. She's the one who's giving it away like candy."

"Her charities give her a connection to the outside world. Writing a check isn't the same as being strong enough to face that world."

The woman Trip had seen wrestling with the dog, the woman who'd come at him with a sword and a rebel yell, wasn't fragile. And the woman he'd kissed certainly wasn't mentally unstable. "Give your daughter some credit, Mayweather. It's not the way I would have done it, but she was resourceful enough to save herself yesterday, and that night your chauffeur was killed."

Spencer Montgomery smoothed his tie and stood. "The Rich Girl Killer doesn't shoot his victims in the middle of traffic jams."

"Somebody was shooting yesterday." Trip reminded him, "He worked with gang members last year when he was going after Audrey Kline. Maybe he has another ally this time."

"The RGK is hands-on." The detective continued to quote his by-the-book profile of the man he was hunting. "His failure with Miss Kline is fueling his pursuit of Charlotte. He likes to terrorize, torture and strangle. He's methodical and precise—very much an in-your-face kind of killer. I believe he suffers from an obsessive-compulsive disorder and perceives that these wealthy young women have wronged him somehow. He's exacting punishment. He's coming. He can't help himself."

Laura Austin-Mayweather's shocked gasp pretty much summed up the growing tension in the room. These people were talking about ongoing cases and estate security, placing blame and deflecting accusations. He was talking about one woman. "He's already here. If you're so smart, Montgomery, tell me—how do you plan to identify your killer and catch him before he succeeds in his quest?"

The detective's light-colored eyes barely blinked. He'd be a tough one to go up against in a poker game. "We were misled by the gang involvement when he went after Miss Kline. But we know how he works now. We set up twenty-four-hour surveillance on Miss Mayweather, tap her phones and the security cameras here. Any time he calls we need to keep him talking as long as possible to help us pinpoint a location, or get some clue to his identity. The next time he delivers a message or tries to approach her, in any disguise, we'll be ready."

"That's your plan? First, she's too fragile, and now you're using Charlotte as bait?"

"I hope that we can assemble evidence from enough of these stalking incidents to piece together their source—where he's getting his inside information on these women. We find the common link and we can zero in on him."

Trip scrubbed his hand over his jaw, not believing what he was hearing. "So you're hoping this bastard terrorizes Charlotte long enough before killing her so that you can find your answers?"

"It's a difficult choice, but I'll be saving lives in the long run."

"You're not saving hers." Trip turned to Jackson. "And you support this idiotic idea?"

"If we don't find a way to catch him, my daughter will die—if not by his hand, then by driving her mad. I nearly lost her once—when she came back from those kidnappers, she was broken. I won't let that happen again."

Just a few long strides took Trip around the table and put him in Montgomery's face. "How do you protect Charlotte when your unsub is living or working or regularly visiting in the same house where she lives? She has a fear of strangers. But how does she identify the enemy when all of your suspects are people she knows? How do *you?* She'll be dead in her locked-up room before you figure it out."

The huffing noise of a panting dog made Trip's heart sink.

He spotted the red glasses and muddy jeans as soon as Charlotte appeared in the archway to the dining room. Max sat beside her, his leash held in a white-knuckled grip. She'd heard every word out of his big, stupid mouth. "Interesting plan. Maybe someone should ask me first."

"AND YOU WONDER WHY I have trust issues. Now I can't even mourn in peace."

Trip stood at the bathroom door watching Charlotte, leaning over the edge of the tub, rinsing the last of the mud and suds from Max's fur. Her bottom bobbed up and down as she moved, and he rolled his eyes away so he could concentrate on the discussion and not the distraction of all those curves emphasized by her clingy wet clothes. The woman really did have a seriously sweet figure, and a surprisingly sharp tongue for someone the rest of the world considered an introvert.

"I can't believe it, all of you eating breakfast, plotting ways to intensify my nightmare or even get me killed."

"I was the one defending you in there."

She shut off the water and warned Max to stay put. "Because I'm too incompetent to defend myself?"

"Because you weren't there." Trip picked up one of the towels stacked on the toilet lid and handed it to her. She wrapped the towel around Max and rocked back on her heels as the dog climbed out of the tub. "Personally, I think Montgomery's plan sucks. There has to be more investigating he can do, more suspects he can bring in, more clues he can uncover before resorting to surveilling you and hoping something new breaks on the case."

Max licked her face while she toweled him dry— the perfect excuse for not making eye contact with him, the perfect barrier for keeping Trip at a distance. "Detective Montgomery told me he's been investigating the RGK murders for two years now. I suppose he's getting desperate. He must be if he thinks I can help him."

"You don't have to do this, Charlotte. Your father thinks catching the killer is the only way to save your life. But I don't think he fully realizes the risk he's taking."

"And you do?"

"You do, too." She was the only person in this house who'd been the victim of a violent crime. She knew better than any one of her well-meaning family the emotional and potentially deadly price they were asking of her. "Tell them no."

Charlotte's cheeks paled at the grim reminder.

But her only response was to let the dog loose. The dog took two steps and shook himself from nose to tail, spraying water all over the bathroom—and Trip's uniform. Point made. Discussion over. Shut up, already.

Or not. After letting out the stopper in the tub, Charlotte picked up a second towel and crawled around the bathroom, wiping splatters of water off the cabinets, walls and fixtures. "You said I could change things. That I didn't have to be afraid the rest of my life."

"I didn't mean this." Trip stepped aside to let the dog trot into the sitting room to find a warm spot on the rug to take a nap.

"How then?" Charlotte shifted her attention to the floor, mopping up the trail Max had made across the tiles. "One thing I agree with Detective Montgomery on is that this sicko will come after me again. He'll leave a note or make a call—I haven't revisited everything that happened during my kidnapping yet, and he's enjoying the game too much. It's like he was there. But those men are all in prison. How can he know so much about those weeks I was a hostage? Why is he doing this to me?"

"Charlotte." Trip knelt down and pulled the towel from her hand.

She snatched the towel right back and kept working. "If I'm the one he'll make contact with, then maybe I should help capture him. That's being strong, isn't it? I'd be taking control of my life, instead of the life outside these doors controlling me. Right?"

"It's a crapshoot. I wasn't talking about risking your life yesterday."

Her hands stilled for a moment and she looked straight at him. "But catching him would make him stop, right?"

Oh, God. Those had better not be tears glinting in her eyes. Now Trip was the one rocking back on his heels as her pain, her bravery, her desperation twisted something deep inside him. But this was a woman he couldn't lie to. "I think the threats will only escalate until we arrest him or—"

"—he kills me."

"I don't like that option."

Trip's husky whisper held her attention for one hushed, intimate moment in time.

And then she reached beneath her glasses to wipe the moisture from her eyes and resumed her work on the floor. "That's why Dad is paying you to be my bodyguard, isn't it?"

"I work for KCPD, not your father."

After a brief hesitation, she ran the towel over the toes of his boots, drying the water droplets off them as well. "So I'm just a plain ol' citizen of K.C. that you've sworn to protect and serve. Just like anyone else."

He finally realized that all her cleaning was busy-work, avoidance of him. And he very much wanted her attention. He needed to touch her and have her be okay with it. He took the towel away and tossed it on top of the hamper. Then, with a hand beneath each elbow, he rose, pulling her to her feet in front of him. "Honey, there's nothing plain or old or like anyone else about you. I'm here because you're in danger. I wouldn't be doing my job if I let you get hurt."

"There are plenty of guards around here. Dad hires the best."

Her hands hovered in the space between them before finally, cautiously, coming to rest at the placket of his black uniform shirt. He liked that, feeling the gentle heat of her fingers seeping through the crisp material to warm his skin.

He dared to pull her closer, to turn her cheek into the pillow of his chest and wrap his arms around her. He rested his chin at the crown of her wild silky curls and savored the small victory of feeling her lean against him. The smells of wet dog and shampoo didn't matter. Damp clothes soaking into his didn't matter. Holding Charlotte mattered. Feeling her softness—under his chin, against his body, in his arms—mattered.

Trip felt stronger, yet oddly more vulnerable when Charlotte snuggled against him like this. Purely masculine instincts were stirring behind his zipper at the decadent sensations of heavy breasts and generous hips fitting up against his harder frame. Yet something scarier and completely unexpected was waking deeper inside him at the fragile trust she was showing by simply letting him hold her.

At least, he hoped it was trust. He prayed it was the beginnings of trust—and not some fear of what he might do if she resisted that allowed him to hold and inhale and feel and touch. That notion alone kept him from tightening his arms around her the way every sensitized cell in his skin yearned to. The idea that Charlotte wasn't completely sure that his attraction to her was genuine kept his hands securely in the middle of her back instead of sliding up to test the weight of a luscious breast or dipping down to that sweet bottom to pull her more firmly into his masculine heat.

Instead, he rubbed his cheek against the caress of her hair and whispered into her ear. "You need someone from the outside looking after you. Because the threat is right here, in this house. We just can't see it. I want to look after you."

He didn't mind when she curled her fingers more tightly into his shirt, pinching a bit of skin underneath. She was holding on, moving closer. "Don't take away the one place I feel secure, Trip. I need my things, my work, my routine."

"That doesn't have to change. I won't ask you to go to a safe house." It would be a hell of a lot safer and easier to defend than leaving her to serve as the bait in her gilded mousetrap. But he hadn't had any luck convincing Detective Montgomery or Jackson Mayweather. He doubted he'd have any more success making Charlotte see reason. So that left plan B. "But I will ask you to let me be a part of that routine."

"You've already barged your way in to my rooms and my life. It's not like I can stop you."

He reluctantly leaned back, leaving his hands at the curve of her waist. She tipped her head up, tilting her gaze at him over the top of her glasses. Her eyes were storm-cloud gray, turbulent with questions and wary suspicion.

Yeah, *that* was the look he needed to get off his conscience and out of his head.

"Oh yes, you can." A little frown appeared between her golden brows, telling him that his response confused her. But he wasn't going to explain what he barely understood himself. Trip pushed her glasses up onto the bridge of her nose, masking her eyes before releasing her. "I'm asking you to let me stay. Let me be a part of your life until we get this guy. I promise I'll keep you safe. Or I'll die trying."

She crossed her arms and drifted back a step. "I thought the whole idea behind a SWAT cop was to keep people from dying."

He didn't laugh. "Let me stay. Trust me, Charlotte. Please."

"Why does it have to be your personal mission to protect me if Dad isn't paying you?"

Guilty conscience? A very real fear that no one else fully perceived the danger she was in? Those big gray eyes that haunted his waking thoughts and dreams? "Let's just say, you'd be doing me a favor."

"I don't understand."

"I'm not sure I do, either. But I don't think I could stand it if you got hurt and I could have done something to stop it."

"I said you didn't have to prove anything—"

Screw patience. Trip caught her face between his hands and pulled her up onto her toes, covering her mouth with his—silencing the excuses she used to push him away, silencing the frustrated need simmering inside him, silencing his own fears that he was growing way too attached to a woman he was completely wrong for.

He pressed his thumb to the swell of her bottom lip, coaxing her to part her lips for him, taking advantage of her warmth and sweetness when she did. Charlotte's fingers crept up around his wrists, holding on as he plunged his tongue inside her mouth to introduce himself to hers. She answered back, her tongue chasing his as he learned each taste and curve. A husky moan, deep in her throat, quickened his pulse as surely as the graze of her curious lips across the jut of his chin. His blood hammered in his veins and pooled in all sorts of achy places when her fingers moved up higher, settling against his jaw and guiding his mouth back to hers as she sampled one lip, then two, then pushed them apart to touch her tongue to the softer skin inside.

Trip wound his arms around her, temptation taking his fingers down to the delicious curve of her bottom and lifting her into the full tutelage of his kiss. She opened for him, welcomed him, taught him a thing or two about the benefits of curiosity and enthusiasm when it came to assuaging and fueling needs like this. He slid a supporting arm around her waist and dropped one hand lower, cupping a buttock that perfectly fit the size of his hand.

It was only when he felt two pert nipples brushing against his chest and the need to take her down to the floor right here in the john surged through him that Trip remembered that business and safety had to come before pleasure. Scaring her off with his baser needs was one risk he could avoid, so with a reluctantly determined gasp for saner air, he summoned the strength to pull her fingers from his neck and lift his mouth from her full, pinkened lips. "Whoa. Whoa, honey. We need to slow down."

Her eyes were dark and hooded and sexy with an innocent desire as she peeked over the top of her glasses at him. He pushed her glasses back into place, making sure to keep his eyes glued to hers and not to the tempting rise and fall of breasts as she crossed her arms beneath them and retreated. "Why do you keep doing that?"

Trip's next several breaths came as deeply and erratically as hers. "Seriously? I didn't think our second makeout session in your father's home with everything else going on around us was the best time or place to go all the way."

"All the way?" Her cheeks blanched a shocked shade of pale. "I meant, why do you keep kissing *me?*"

Ah, hell. Another encounter with Charlotte Mayweather had just taken a sharp turn into crazy land, and suddenly he was the bad guy again. "I don't know. Why do you kiss me back?"

"Because you're an overwhelming presence and apparently it's hard to get rid of you when you put your mind to something."

He scrubbed his hand over his mouth and jaw, and squared off against what sounded a lot like an accusation. "Like wanting to kiss you? Like feeling something and acting on it? I'm a healthy male and a human being, and you are gettin' into my head in ways that make me want to…" *Pull out my hair? Protect you? Bed you?* Maybe he was the one riding on the crazy train. "What do you want me to say? How do I get you to believe in me?"

"Trip, you can probably guess that I don't have a lot of experience with men. The truth is, I have no experience. At all. I don't know how to kiss."

"Then you're a natural talent."

That made her blush.

"I've never had sex. I don't know how to make a relationship work. I don't know if I even can." She shook her head, scattering toffee curls around her face as she retreated another step. "I'm not used to feeling or kissing or needing or whatever it is you want from me."

Frustration gave way to something infinitely more tender, and Trip found his patience again. "I want all those things from you. But only if you're willing to give them."

"I am feeling something for you, Trip. But do you have any idea how much that scares me?" She tucked a curl behind her ear, but it sprang back out to fall on her cheek. "I need to feel safe. In all things."

"I said I've got your back." He caught the independent curl with the tip of his finger and smoothed it back into place, then leaned down to press a kiss to her temple. "In this, too. Just give me a chance to show you I'm not the bad guy here. If I say or do anything you don't like, you tell me."

His body could scream away in protest if denying any physical or emotional need for this woman is what it took to see trust shining in her eyes.

Maybe it was time to go back to proving that. He pulled his hand away and turned into the sitting room. "You don't have to worry about any *us* right now. Finish drying the dog and get his collar and leash. You said you wanted to go to the cemetery? Let me call the rest of my team. We'll get you away from this house for a little while.

"You're under KCPD's watch now."

Chapter Eight

Charlotte knelt down to lay the bouquet of roses on the turned-up mound of earth beside the flowers that had once been draped over Richard's coffin. Max came over to sniff her handiwork and she scratched his head before shooing him on his way to follow the path of some squirrel or rabbit that'd come through earlier. She kissed her fingers and touched them to the plastic marker that held Richard's name and dates until a permanent stone monument could be fixed into place, knowing it was as close to trading a hug with him as she could ever get again.

"Thank you, my friend. For everything. I'm sorry. So sorry." Tears burned in her sinuses and squeezed out through the rapid blink of her lashes to warm her cheeks in the cooling air.

In the middle of the spring afternoon it felt like twilight. A storm was brewing overhead again, filling the sky with fast-moving clouds. Tall oaks and pine trees dotted each side of the road that twisted up through the hills of Mt. Washington Cemetery, their thick trunks and budding branches casting long shadows over her. But no shadow seemed as tall and foreboding as the sturdy bulk of Trip Jones standing beside her, with a handgun strapped to his thigh, a military-looking rifle draped in the crook of his elbow and a stone-cold expression of wary alertness stamped onto his rugged features.

"You okay?" Trip's voice rumbled down on the breeze that was picking up.

Charlotte huddled inside her trench coat and the body armor Trip had insisted she wear, and slowly stood. "He should have been retired, enjoying his grandchildren. He shouldn't have died because some freak wanted to get to me."

She saw Trip's black-gloved hand leave his rifle and reach for her. But just before he touched the small of her back, he curled his fingers into his palm and tapped at the headset hooked to his ear instead. "How are we doing?"

A chorus of "clears" and one "nothing here" answered loudly enough for Charlotte to hear.

Captain Cutler buzzed in as well. "Easy, people. Keep your eyes open. We're not in any rush here."

But Trip apparently was. He moved a couple of steps along the trail Max had taken, then circled around to stand beside her again. His hazel eyes stopping scanning their surroundings long enough to land on her. "Are you ready to head back?"

With his truck in the shop, Trip had driven her to

Mt. Washington in one of the team's SUVs, which was parked at the foot of the hill, while the others had followed behind them in an imposing armored SWAT van. It was parked around a bend, out of sight beyond a copse of trees, just like the other members of his team remained hidden in the trees and monuments around them.

"I think I've decided how I'm going to honor him." Charlotte murmured the announcement to the flowers and the sign and anyone who might listen. "I'm going to set up a college fund for all his grandchildren. I'll call the bank and our attorneys when I get home."

"Sounds like a good plan to me." He glanced toward the sky. "The storm's about to break. I can feel the dampness in the breeze. We should get home so you can make those calls."

But she wasn't ready to disturb this solemn, secure moment. "Could we stay for a while? Richard was always so patient with me—I don't want to rush my time here. I don't mind a little rain."

"A little?" That stern mouth eased into a grin. Trip's easy capitulation to her request reminded her more of the man who'd kissed her and less of the warrior standing guard. "We've had so much this spring, creeks are flooding, roads are closing— they're sandbagging the levees up by the river."

Charlotte discovered she could smile, too, with the subtle glimpse of Trip's humor. "Washing away is the least of my worries. I used to love playing out in the rain. I think when I was little, I thought I was combining bath time and playtime, meaning I could stay outside longer."

"Why do I get the feeling you were a real handful growing up?"

"Me? An odd duck is more like it. I just spent a lot of time in my head. I was always curious, always reading, always thinking. I suppose I did give my dad a few headaches when I wandered off on one of my adventures and lost track of the time. I didn't become any trouble until after high school."

She shivered and slid her fingers up to her rebuilt ear to finger the gold earring there, her thoughts automatically including prom night and the disastrous events that had changed her life.

This time, his black glove settled at the small of her back. "Chilly?"

"I'm okay." At first she stiffened at his touch, unsure of its motive. Comfort? Protection? Keeping her focused on the conversation? Years of shielding herself from anyone outside her family made it difficult to resolve this growing fascination with Trip's passion and strength and almost poignant patience with her. He liked to touch and she…liked him touching her. But despite the fretful anticipation his sheer masculinity and straightforward desire seemed to have awakened in her, it took a huge leap of faith to admit she was developing feelings for this man she'd known for a week. Her body's instincts to seek warmth and shelter let her relax and turn her cheek into his chest.

But her mind, her emotions, insisted on holding something back. In some ways, she knew as little about men as she knew a lot about archaeology. Boys hadn't looked at her as dating material in school, and she hadn't looked at men in that way since. There was a security in being able to shut off her feelings, knowing that was one aspect of her life she could control—no one could mock or hurt her, no one could trick or abuse her. Yet there was a loneliness in that particular skill, too, and she was just beginning to wonder whether it left her in a more perfect prison than all her phobias put together did.

Trip's fingers tightening at the nip of her waist encouraged her to stay in the moment and continue. "I loved to read mysteries, solve puzzles. But I was just as interested in climbing trees and exploring whatever new places I could get myself into—a friend's attic, the museum's back rooms."

"So you've always been the explorer."

"It wasn't like I had any dates to keep me busy. I had my friends, my homework, my adventures…I guess I always did march to the beat of my own drum."

"High school's a tough place to be different, isn't it?"

Charlotte nodded against the rough weave of his

vest cover. She had an idea he was referring to his own experience about being labeled for his brawn and learning disability, rather than commiserating over her odd habits and plain looks. But he understood. Maybe more than most people, he understood why she'd made the choices she had. "That's why I was so excited about going to prom. It was my first date that Dad and some social event of his had nothing to do with. Landon Turner. He was a new guy in school my senior year—he had that whole swarthy Italian look going on."

"I hate him already."

She felt the first sprinkle of rain on her cheek, and while the initial drop startled her, she soon savored the cool trickles of moisture on her skin. "He had a soccer scholarship to play on the team with my friend, Harper. I'd been pining after Harper for years, but he never saw beyond the glasses. A buddy of mine, Donny Kemp—he was on the quiz bowl team with me—had asked me first, out of the blue—I didn't really know him, didn't know he even liked me—so I said I needed time to think about it. I guess I was still holding out for a miracle invitation from Harper."

"Sheesh, the soap opera of high-school relationships. I don't miss that."

She tiptoed her fingers up his vest until she found the warmth of skin above Trip's collar to cling to. "I'd been tutoring Landon, to help him keep his grades up so he could stay at Sterling instead of going back to a public high school. When he asked me, I thought it was as close to dating Harper as I was going to get so I said yes. And then I found out he'd done it as an initiation rite. One of the kidnappers had given him a hundred dollars to get me to the school, away from Dad and his security."

"What the hell kind of initiation involves getting you kidnapped?"

Charlotte flinched at the sudden sharpness in Trip's voice and he immediately released her.

"Sorry." He skimmed his hand over his face, but she didn't think he was snarling at the rain wetting his skin. "No wonder you don't trust men."

He turned away, muttering a curse, then startled her when he swung back around to face her. "Did Turner pay for his part in the kidnapping? Does he have any reason to come after you again?"

"He didn't come after me." Her guardian had returned in full force. How did a man turn his compassion and gentleness on and off so quickly? She hugged her arms around her waist, afraid of her own warring needs to run away or offer a reassuring touch. "Landon's prank was a cruel one, but he didn't know about the kidnapping. He testified on my behalf at the trial by identifying the man who'd paid him, and helped get the conviction. He was kicked out of Sterling Academy, and I think lost a couple of college scholarships. But the judge didn't file any criminal charges. He has no reason to want to hurt me now."

"Don't defend him." Charlotte backed away as Trip advanced, his suspicions overriding his patience with her. "If he didn't know about the kidnapping, then how did the kidnappers know about the initiation?"

"All the guys at school knew about the initiation dare. If I'd been more of a social creature, I would have heard the gossip, too. One of them must have let it slip somewhere, and the kidnappers paid Landon to make sure it was me he took that night." Talented though he was with his feet, Landon had never been the brightest bulb at Sterling. "He apologized, over and over. He used to call me…"

Every day. For months.

Charlotte. You have to forgive me. Charlotte? Answer me!

Oh, my God. Had she missed a connection between Landon and her kidnappers? A connection between then and now?

Charlotte's heart rate kicked up a notch. Her breathing went shallow. She was going back in time. Slipping into the past. Remembering. "I want to go home."

"Honey, are you—?"

"Don't 'honey' me!" She whirled around, looking for Max. "Stay in the moment. Stay in the moment," she chanted. "Max?"

"Jones." Captain Cutler's voice buzzed into the radio, loud enough for Charlotte to hear the summons. "Is there a problem up there?"

"Charlotte?"

She put her fingers to her mouth and whistled. "Max!"

"She's on the verge of a panic attack, sir. Call everyone in. We're coming down."

Charlotte yelped at the big hand that closed around her arm.

But it wouldn't let go. "Look at me, Charlotte." He had her by both arms now, had hunkered down so she could see his face. "Look at me."

It was Trip. She knew it was Trip. But she was afraid. Afraid of the calls and the memories and the mistakes she couldn't save herself from. She blinked her eyes into focus. "I need to go home. I want to go home."

"Okay." His grip shifted to one arm and he gentled his tone as he towered over her. "I'm sorry I upset you. Stay in the moment, okay? Stay with me."

"I'm sorry, Trip. I must have pushed myself to be outside a little too long." She felt twenty-five pounds of furry warmth wedge its way in between them and sit on her foot. Max. Thank goodness. She reached down to stroke his fur, taking the edge off her panic. "Good boy, Max."

"You have no idea what a fighter you are, do you?"

"What do you mean?"

"You could summon the troops with that whistle." Trip pulled the dog's leash from her coat pocket and hooked him up. He rubbed Max around his neck and ears before pushing the leash into Charlotte's hand and straightening. "I'm the one who pushed you too hard. I thought Turner might be some kind of break on the case."

"You were just doing your job."

"I was being a jealous idiot and I scared you instead of helping." He held out his hand for her to take. "Let's get you home so you can make those phone calls about Richard's memorial, okay?"

She nodded, wrapping both hands around the leash, unsure what to make of his compliment or apology or the whole idea of a man being jealous over her.

Trip's gaze dropped to her fingers, understanding the unspoken message and accepting it. "And as far as Turner goes?"

"What about him?"

"Innocent or not, he'd better never show his face around me." Backed up by an ominous rumble of thunder overhead, his vow triggered a riot of inexplicable goose bumps across her skin. If they'd been sparked by her usual anxiety or the possessive promise in his words that tickled something new and uniquely feminine inside her, she couldn't yet tell. "Come on. Let's get out of the rain."

Although she hadn't taken his hand, he still put his fingers at her back to position her in front of him and lead the way down the hill with Max. He released her to tap on his radio. "We're heading back to the car. Bring it in, guys."

"That's a negative. Stand fast, big guy." Captain Cutler's crisp voice buzzed over the radio. Charlotte spotted the reason for the warning appearing from behind a mask of trees and doubling back on one of the cemetery's hairpin turns. Her eyes widened. Her steps slowed. "We've got an unmarked vehicle approaching on your six. White van, local plates."

"I see it." Trip's hand clamped down on her shoulder, stopping her beside a red marble headstone. "Let it pass."

Charlotte grabbed hold of the red marble, swaying as the van crept up behind the black SUV.

Her brain spun around inside her skull as Charlotte pushed herself up from the pavement. Where were her glasses? What was happening to her? Was she bleeding?

"Sir, it's slowing down." A woman's voice broke through the static in Charlotte's ears. "All I can see is the driver. One male. Sir, he's puttin' on the brakes."

But Charlotte was slipping back in time.

The screech of tires echoed through her aching head. What was going on? She squinted the blur of white into focus. A van. A white van. She tried to

*push up to her knees, but her head was so heavy. A
yawning black hole opened in the side of the van.
"Get up!"*

*Clarity kicked in a moment too late. There were
hands on her, rough hands pinching and grabbing
and countering every kick and twist she made. "No!
Let go! Don't take me!"*

*"Shut up, Charlotte!" She flew through the air
and landed in a heap on the dirty, rusty floor. She
screamed as a hood came over her head and the
van door slammed shut.*

*They were speeding away as a needle pricked her
arm.*

"Charlotte!"

Someone had pushed her down to her knees and
shoved something warm and furry against her.

"Charlotte, you're all right—stay in the moment."

She fought inside her head to ground herself, to
find her way back to reality. Her pants were wet.
Something cold and wet was soaking into her jeans.
Max. Max had his front paws on her shoulder and
was licking her face. Her hands crept around his
neck, hugging him tight. "Good boy. Good boy,
Max."

"Stay in the moment," the deep voice beside her
commanded. She took a deep, calming breath.

And then she saw the white van. "No."

It stopped at the bottom of the hill. They were
coming.

"I won't go. Don't take me!"

He turned her bruised face into the stale bedding. "I'm tired of waiting for my millions. It's time to show Daddy just how serious we are."

And then she felt the cold scissors squeeze her earlobe. "No!"

"Charlotte!" the voice snapped. "Honey, I don't want to touch you right now. Listen to my voice. Stay in the moment."

"Trip?" She pulled one hand from Max's fur and reached out.

The driver's door opened and a man climbed out of the van. "Charlotte Mayweather?"

He looked right at her. He was coming for her. She backed away.

"I have something for you." He held up a small package wrapped in plastic.

Charlotte answered with a scream.

Chapter Nine

Ignoring the barking dog jumping at his legs, Trip threw his arm around Charlotte and twisted to put himself between her and the perp. He muffled her screams against his chest, pressed his lips against her hair and muttered every apology he could think of as he took her down to the slick wet grass and rolled his body over hers, waiting for the attack.

"Gun?"

"Remote?"

"Bomb?"

He heard the speculation over his radio, heard a slew of curses, then Randy Murdock's harsh, "Drop it! Get down on the ground! Now!"

"Madre de Dios!" Trip turned his head at the thick Latin accent and saw Randy's blond ponytail flying as she kicked aside the package and put the driver on the pavement. "I surrender! I surrender! *Por favor!*"

Murdock hooked her sniper's rifle over her shoulder, put her knee in the man's back and cuffed him.

Captain Cutler pointed his gun at the windshield as Sergeant Delgado approached the rear of the van at rifle-point and swung it open. He paused, climbed inside, then jumped back out to the ground and flattened himself on the road to look beneath the van.

He could read the results in his team's posture even before he heard Delgado's report. "Clear. The van's clear."

"He's clean," Murdock reported, rising after frisking the driver for weapons.

"Let me up." Charlotte's panicked screams had subsided to a hoarse plea. "I'm okay, Trip. I need to see him."

"Not yet." He got around the dog's frantic need to get to his mistress by grabbing him by the collar and pulling him down to the ground beside them. "Clear" wasn't the same as "all clear," and Trip had no intention of any surprises popping out to finish whatever the driver had started.

Captain Cutler lowered his weapon to a forty-five-degree angle and came around the van's front bumper while Sergeant Delgado turned his back to the van and circled, eyeing each direction along the asphalt and into the trees that dropped off to the bottom of the hill across the road. The captain nudged the plastic bag that had tumbled into the ditch with his toe, then knelt beside it.

The dog pushed against Trip's shoulder. Or maybe it was Charlotte. "I can't breathe."

Cutler holstered his gun. "No weapon. I repeat, no weapon." He plucked the bag from the water draining into the brick ditch and stood. "I've got one red-rose corsage with a note attached."

"A note?" Charlotte's breathy terror entered Trip's ear and went straight to the heap of guilt already twisting his gut. "For me?"

"Charming son of a bitch. Let's get this guy up," the captain ordered. "Do you speak English?"

"Yes."

"Did you write this note?"

"No, sir. No, I just deliver."

"Let's get you moving, too." Trip shifted his weight off Charlotte and rolled to his feet, bracing as he pulled her up in the same movement. "The RGK used a bomb when he went after Audrey last year," he explained, suspecting an apology alone wouldn't erase the wide-eyed shock behind Charlotte's glasses. "I wasn't taking any chances of a replay of that attack. And after shooting at my truck, I'm not waiting to see if he graduates to real bullets. Are you hurt? Are you with me?"

She had one hand on her ear, the other clutched tightly around Max's leash. Her eyes were transfixed by the van, but hopefully not focused in the past.

He'd protected her like the cop he was trained to be. But it was the man in him who cupped her cheek in his gloved hand and tilted her face up into the rain. "Charlotte?"

The rain splashed on her glasses, making her blink. Then some of the haze cleared away and she slowly shook her head. "I'm not hurt."

But she was still rubbing her ear. Had she hit her head on the way down? "Honey?"

He pushed her hand away and brushed aside her hair. Her earring was missing.

"Don't."

She jerked away, but he'd already seen it. The jagged line. The tiny white scars and stiff molded skin. She'd lost part of her ear and plastic surgeons had rebuilt it. No wonder she was so sensitive about him touching her there.

"Honey, I..." But the stamp of her features warned him she didn't want an apology. A quick scan up the hill a few feet led him to the gold earring. She snatched it from his hand and clipped it back on. "Are you with me?"

This time she nodded. She wiped the rain from her glasses and looked him in the eye. "The kidnappers took me in a white van. I was flashing back."

"I suspected as much." How could a woman he wanted to reach for so badly not welcome his touch? He had to remind himself that protecting Charlotte wasn't about what *he* needed, and he curled his needy fingers into his palm. "Can you walk? Stick close. I intend to find out what this guy wants."

Trip tried not to read too much into Charlotte capturing his hand and holding on with both of hers as he led her down the hill. Yeah, maybe she was more scared of her stalker and the rest of the world than she was of him right now, but that didn't mean she wasn't still afraid of his big, bad self barging into her life and into her personal space.

He wasn't ready to let go, either. He raised his voice, not needing the radio to communicate. "What's in the note?"

Captain Cutler assessed Charlotte's condition before handing over the package. His curse matched the captain's. Charlotte didn't need to see this.

Don't despair, Charlotte. You'll be joining your old friends soon. Not even your new friends can stop the inevitable. I'm counting the days until we're together for the last time.

"A red rose with silver ribbons. That's the corsage I had at prom. I dropped it in the parking lot before I was abducted." Charlotte's hands pumped his. "What does it say?"

"Uh-uh."

The stubborn woman snatched it from his hands and read it, anyway. "Oh, my God."

He took the vile message from her and handed it back to the captain. "Our guy's a voyeur. He's around here somewhere, watching her reaction to this." While the captain dispatched Murdock up the hill to get the best recon of the cemetery, Trip pulled the pale-faced driver away from the van and turned him so Charlotte could get a good look at him. "You know this guy?"

"No."

"*Señor, por favor.*" The stocky driver was younger than Trip had first suspected. He was guessing by the thickness of his accent that he hadn't been in the country for very long, either.

Trip pressed further. "He doesn't work for you or your family?"

"I don't know. He's not anyone I recognize."

"Please, sir. I work for the florist." He pointed over his shoulder to the road leading toward the cemetery's north entrance. "I deliver flowers to the Gonzalez funeral down at the chapel."

"The back of the van's empty," Delgado pointed out.

The driver turned to him, as if that proved his innocence. "I already go to the chapel. I'm on my way back to my uncle's shop now."

"Then you're taking the scenic route."

The driver frowned, not understanding Delgado's sarcasm.

Trip wanted answers. "What are you doing up here? With this?"

"The man. The man at the chapel—he give me fifty dollars to take this up the hill to the lady with the dog." With his cuffed hands the driver pushed the corsage bag away from him. "I give it. Please, *señor*—I good man."

The unexpected opportunity to put an end to this fueled Trip's adrenaline. "He could still be at the chapel."

Cutler nodded. "Sarge, take the car and check it out."

Delgado caught the keys Trip tossed him. "What are the chances he's still there?"

"If he's gone, then you find me footprints, tire tracks, something we can follow. I don't like having a serial killer with so many ties to my team. And I don't think we're just talking about Alex anymore, are we?" His sharp blue eyes didn't miss a detail, darting down to the clasp of Trip and Charlotte's hands. "We're going to wind up having a showdown one of these days, and I'd rather we capture him before he catches us off guard."

Amen to that.

Delgado revved the engine and turned a U-ie on the narrow road, speeding down toward the chapel.

"I'll bag this and call the detectives." Captain Cutler adjusted the bill of his cap as the sky darkened and the rain changed from a few sprinkles to a steady downpour. He opened the van door and urged the driver to climb back inside and slide across to the passenger seat. "I'll keep an eye on this guy until we hear from Sarge, see if I can get any kind

of a description out of him to back up his story."
He nodded toward Charlotte, his face reflecting the
same wary concern Trip felt. "Put her in our truck
and stay with her."

Trip was anxious to get Charlotte behind the van's
armored walls as well as out of view of the psycho-
pervert who was behind this sick game. "I don't like
the coincidence of that van showing up when we're
here with Charlotte."

Cutler agreed. "Me, either. Who knew that you
were bringing her to the cemetery?"

Charlotte seemed to startle from some deep
thought when they looked to her for an answer. "I
always tell Dad when I leave the estate. Laura and
Kyle were with him in his office, meeting with the
event planner they've been working with, Jeffrey
Beecher. Bailey was there, too. My stepmother wants
to host a fundraiser for the city's botanical gardens
once all this rain clears."

"Plus there are the security guards and Detective Montgomery and whoever he's got watching
the cameras to track Charlotte's every move there,"
Trip added.

"Well, that certainly narrows down the list of suspects."

The captain's sarcasm wasn't lost on Trip. "Believe
me, you don't know what kind of traffic that place
gets."

"Then I'd get her out of there."

"I would, too. Unfortunately, it's not up to me."

"Do the best you can, Trip. Trust your instincts—they're good ones. SWAT Team One will back you up as much as we can."

"Thank you, sir."

Trip was already turning Charlotte down the road toward the SWAT truck, keeping his chest aligned with her back and his eyes peeled as Cutler climbed into the white van.

"This way." He stopped her and pointed into the trees. "It'll be quicker if we cut through."

She stepped off the asphalt with him, but put on the brakes when she got a peek over the edge to the road below. "That's a pretty steep drop-off, and I can hear how fast and full the creek is running from up here."

"Yeah, but I hate being out in the open like this." Trip plowed into her back at the abrupt halt, knocking her forward, but catching her before she tumbled. "Anyone could drive by. I feel like there are eyes on us." He took advantage of his arm being around her waist and pulled her back against him, savoring the contact with her hips and thighs against his, needing it to feel she was secure. "It'll take us ten minutes to follow the road around, and if that sicko is here, you'd be in easy view the whole way. The shortcut will take us five and give us cover, if you're willing to get your shoes muddy. The trees should give us enough handholds to control our descent."

For a moment she relaxed against him, completing the embrace. But then she was taking his hand, clicking to the dog and sliding down to the first tree. "I need to learn to keep myself safe, too. We're cutting through."

Four minutes and only one foot in the creek later, Trip was lifting Charlotte into the back of the SWAT van. Max just needed an invitation to join them, and after the dog hopped up and shook off, Trip closed and locked the door behind them. While Max found a spot on the floor to curl up and give himself a bath, Trip sat Charlotte on the bench that ran parallel of the center aisle and scooted past them to make sure the doors up front were locked. Then he secured the cage between the cab and the supply and command center of the truck. With inches of reinforced steel and no way to see in between Charlotte and her stalker, Trip finally relaxed his guard and breathed a little easier.

But the air inside the van quickly filled with the dank smells of mud and dog and grass stains on their clothes. And there was something warm and intimate about their bodies moving in the close confines of the narrow passageway. Charlotte's clothes were rumpled and sticking to every generous curve as she peeled off her Kevlar, but her cheeks were flushed with a healthy color and her eyes were bright with relief as she pulled off her glasses and reached beneath her black trench coat to find the hem of her blouse to dry her lenses.

As he stowed his rifle, three things hit Trip with stunning clarity. One, Charlotte Mayweather possessed a surprising beauty that was far more enticing than she gave herself credit for.

Two, Captain Cutler was right—he was feeling something for her more profound than guilt or some need to prove that her first impression of him as a man she needed to fear was wrong. He wouldn't be tamping down these warring needs of wanting to wrap her in his arms to shield her from everything she had to fear, and wanting to kiss that pursed mouth and uncover her layer by layer to get inside her if that was the case, right?

And three, as much as Charlotte's complexities both baffled and fascinated him, as much as he suspected her complete acceptance of him would finally give him the solace he sought to ease the physical and emotional hunger she'd awakened inside him, Trip knew he wasn't the right man for her. Not in the long run.

Charlotte needed Mr. Sensitive, not a hands-on kind of cowboy who wrestled her to the ground and dragged her through the mud and kissed her when she rankled him as he did. She needed someone well-educated and refined enough to live in her world, not a man who couldn't manage a cup and saucer and who took four months to read a book that a woman like her could finish in a week. She could use him as a cop, as the protector he was. But without the RGK in her life, she'd have no place for him—no use for a bull like him in her china shop of a world.

When he turned around and watched her fix her glasses and brave face back into place, that last realization hit him hard in the gut—and maybe closer to something a little more vital. He was falling hard and fast for the quirky heiress. But how the hell could the two of them together ever work?

"What?"

Smooth, big guy. Real smooth. She'd caught him staring, with maybe a little too much hunger and desperation stamped on his face.

He pulled off his gloves, shook off the excess moisture and stuffed them into his pocket. "Sorry I made you do the wilderness trek like that. I guess I've forced you to do a lot of stuff you're not comfortable with lately."

She shrugged off his apology. "Trust me, I'm happier being indoors and out of sight sooner rather than later."

"I'll get you home as soon as Captain Cutler calls with an 'all clear.'"

Her slight smile surprised him. "You're certainly an adventure to hang out with. I don't know that being soaked straight through to my backside is what I'd call fun, but about fifteen years ago, I'd have been all over sliding down that hillside and climbing the rocks across the creek. About the only dirt I get my hands on now is the dust at the museum."

"You know, you like getting dirty more than any reclusive heiress I know."

For one moment her eyes narrowed in a confused frown. And then she laughed. "So you've met a lot of us?"

"You're pretty when you smile, Charlotte."

And then her cell phone rang. Not the one Spencer Montgomery had bagged as evidence from the museum. Not the one Bud Preston had retrieved from the limo. The brand-new cell phone someone on her father's staff had picked up for her that morning was ringing.

The smile had vanished. "Maybe it's someone else. Like Audrey. We haven't talked since Alex put her under twenty-four-hour guard."

"She has the new number?" They both knew the timing was suspect after the note and van and corsage.

She pulled the cell from her coat pocket and stared at the blinking light. "It says 'Unknown Caller.' I have to answer it, don't I? That's what Detective Montgomery said."

Trip rested his hand on her shoulder and sat on the bench beside her. "Put it on speakerphone."

With a jerky nod, she answered it. "Hello?"

"Did you like my gift, Charlotte? Brings back fun memories, doesn't it?"

Trip snatched the phone from her fingers and spun away. "You better hope to hell you and I never come face-to-face, pal."

But while Trip seethed, the bastard didn't so much as startle. He breathed softly and then said, "Put Charlotte back on the phone."

"No."

"Then I'll call her again. And again. And again. On this number or another one. Until she gets my message personally."

As much as he wanted to hang up, Trip knew the longer they kept this psycho talking, the more chances they had at him slipping up and giving them a clue to his identity or location. But he didn't want her to hear this. He didn't want her to be afraid.

Trip felt four fingers curl beneath his belt at the back of his waist. Charlotte's unexpected touch took the edge off his protective anger. Did she have any idea how brave she really was? He dropped his arm around her shoulders and when she didn't pull away, he hugged her close. She curled her arms around his waist and answered. "I'm here. Why are you doing this?"

"You always prided yourself in being so smart, Charlotte. But it's driving you nuts that you can't figure it out, isn't it?"

"Is that the idea? To drive me nuts?"

"It's hard to keep it all together and move on with the life you want when someone else is calling the shots, don't you think?"

Her hair rustled against Trip's vest when she shook her head. "I don't understand. I've never done anything wrong. I've never hurt anyone."

"That's what you and your friends all claim. Yet one by one you've all denied me what I wanted, what I deserved. I paid a terrible price for your betrayal. Justice is finally being served."

"My friends? You killed Val and Gretchen? You tried to kill Audrey?"

"I'm going to kill you, too, sweetheart. Make sure your boyfriend hears that." Trip could make out the sound of a finely tuned engine revving in the background. The perv was on the road, on the move. "No wealthy bitch will ever say 'no' to me again. I'm going to kill you, too."

Trip closed the phone and stuffed it into his pocket as soon as the call disconnected. Then he gathered Charlotte into his arms and squeezed her tight, feeling her shaking. Or maybe he was the one shaking.

But as Charlotte wound her arms around his waist and nestled under his chin, he felt his own fears dissipating, his anger hardening into something primal and territorial. "He's not going to hurt you, honey. I swear it."

"Because you've got my back?"

"Yeah." He tunneled his fingers into her rain-softened curls and buried his nose in their fragrant scent. "I'm calling the captain and then Spencer Montgomery. They need to know about this call. I think I can get a general idea what kind of vehicle he was driving from the sound of the engine."

"And tell Captain Cutler the man he has in custody isn't the man who's been calling me. The guy in the van has much too thick of an accent."

"Look at us, narrowing down the list of suspects." But there was nothing funny about eliminating one man out of hundreds of possibilities for the Rich Girl Killer.

"Trip?"

"I know. You want to go home."

Her fingers snuck up to his jaw and an answering heat pulsed to that spot. And then she touched his lips, lightly dancing over them with her fingertips as if trying to recall what they'd felt like pressed against hers. He groaned deep in his chest, his whole body aching to answer that sweetly curious caress. But she was leaning back, tugging at his chin, asking him to look at her. Easily and willingly done. "Only if you're there, too. I know I keep freaking out on you, but I think I need you. Will you stay with me until this is over?"

The trust wasn't there in her eyes. Not yet. But he wasn't about to give her any reason to doubt him.

"Try pushing me away. This boy don't budge."

HIS HANDS WERE SHAKING as he tucked the phone inside his jacket pocket. What the hell? That conversation had lasted longer than the sixty seconds of toying with Charlotte that he normally allowed himself.

He'd lost his temper. That big bozo cop who thought he was on some personal mission to shadow Charlotte's every move had interfered with the plan and made him lose his temper.

The rear end of a semi loomed up at an alarming speed and he jerked the steering wheel to the left, not caring about the honking horn that warned him he'd cut someone off in the passing lane. He flew another two miles on I-435 before finally getting a glimpse of his own reflection in the rearview mirror.

"What are you doing?" he asked, reassured by the intelligence looking back at him. "Why are you letting them get to you again?"

Taking a deep cleansing breath, he slowed the car to a legal speed and merged with the traffic that would take him into one of the wealthiest neighborhoods in Kansas City, south of the downtown area near the Plaza. He was expected shortly, and he hated to be late. He might have to bite his tongue about some things for now, but in the end, he'd be victorious and they'd be the ones groveling for mercy.

He'd been beaten and talked down to, denied his family, rejected and overlooked because of those women. It wasn't right for a man to endure all he had. There had to be retribution. Someone had to pay—as dearly as he had—in order to restore the balance that his world so desperately needed.

As he slowed down for a stoplight, he reached across the seat and picked up his camera. He brought up his most recent pictures on the digital screen and smiled.

Nice. Spying the florist delivery van and putting it to good use while he'd been following her trip to the old man's grave had been a stroke of pure genius. The driver had been more than willing to help for fifty bucks. He might have driven up to Charlotte for free once he'd turned on the sob story about being an old boyfriend who wanted to show he still cared for his grieving ex.

"Look at the fear on your face, Charlotte." If her big armed buddy hadn't been there with the dog, she would have wigged out completely.

Having the cop join the conversation on the phone wasn't exactly what he'd wanted, but it was satisfying to hear the wobble in Charlotte's tone, even with her protector there with her. That meant he was well and truly inside her head now. Very nice.

When the turn signal for the next lane came on, he shut down the camera and carefully returned it to the pocket of the rolled-up coveralls in the gym bag beside him. He zipped the bag shut, then neatly arranged the handles so that they hung evenly on each side of the bag. For a moment, he contemplated giving in to the urge to pull his cigarettes from the bag's side pocket. But he would be meeting people too soon, and he couldn't afford to have the telltale scent of tobacco on him.

The light changed and he accelerated through the intersection, smiling at his success today, formulating the details for his next encounter with Charlotte. He had to get her alone to carry out the final phase of his plan. He couldn't risk her snapping out of her delusions. That meant taking care of the dog. And getting her away from the cop.

He drove over the bridge at Brush Creek, idly noting how the water was rushing near the top of the concrete walkways on each bank. Another few inches of rain, and parts of downtown K.C. could be blocked by flash flooding and closed streets. He could use that to his advantage. Yes, that might be exactly the best way to isolate Charlotte from her bodyguards.

His blood hummed at the sweet, sweet anticipation of his revenge. He wanted Charlotte Mayweather screaming and shattered and begging for mercy when he squeezed the life from her throat.

He smiled. Val dead. Gretchen dead. Audrey sequestered under lock and key. And soon, Charlotte would be dead.

The four women who'd ruined his life, who'd treated him as a second-class citizen unworthy of their time and consideration. He was better than that.

Better than them. Soon, they'd all be dead and his hunger for their suffering would be appeased.

And then he could finally put his demons to rest.

Chapter Ten

"Another call?" Charlotte let her stepbrother, Kyle, hug his arm around her and walk her to his chair at the end of the dining room table. "How are you holding up?"

"I'm sorry." She patted his arm as he knelt beside her, then looked to her father, who was pushing away from the head of the table and hurrying toward her. "I didn't mean to interrupt your dinner. I just wanted to let you know that I was home and I was safe."

Her gaze automatically went to the big man standing in the archway between the dining room and foyer. Even separated from the group of family hurrying over to give her hugs and words of reassurance, he dominated the room with his steely eyes and alert, warriorlike stance. He moved aside only when the butler announced Spencer Montgomery's arrival and the emotionless, red-haired detective strode into the room to question her.

"There was a written threat, too," she added,

a few minutes later, reading the details Detective Montgomery was listing in his notebook.

He nodded, clicking his pen and tucking it back inside the pocket of his blazer. "I got that and the flower from Captain Cutler. Plus, the name of the florist van driver. I don't think there's any reason to hold Mr. Gutierrez, although I did ask him to meet with one of our sketch artists to see if we can get a physical description of the man who paid him to accost you like that. We'll see if he shows up. His documentation was a little sketchy and," he glanced over his shoulder at Trip, still standing watch, "for some reason he's a little leery of the police right now."

Trip offered no apology. "We had no idea who he was. We weren't going to let him get to Charlotte."

And she, for one, was more and more glad that she did have SWAT Team One's personal protection. She offered Trip a quick, grateful smile, but turned her attention back to the detective. She was anxious to finish the report, get out of the sticky, muddy clothes that were drying against her skin and get to the soothing solitude of her rooms. "Someone is doing his damnedest to re-create every detail of the kidnapping. All I need is for that creep to actually put his hands on me and the nightmare will be complete."

Her father, hovering behind her chair, leaned over

to kiss the crown of her hair. "No. That will not happen."

Her stepsister, Bailey, who'd been sitting kitty-corner from her throughout the interview, squeezed her hand. "Maybe we should postpone the garden party for a while, until all this blows over."

Spencer Montgomery eyed her straight across the table as if she was as airy as a piece of strawberry fluff. "This is a serial killer we're talking about, not the weather. It won't just blow over."

Bailey bristled in her pale pink suit, but met the detective's faintly condescending gaze with a tilt of her chin. "I'm talking about Char's comfort, not your investigation. She doesn't like large crowds of people, and I don't see why we should add to her stress when this situation is already difficult enough for her."

Trip added a grumpy echo from the doorway. "Finally, a voice of reason."

Bailey wilted under the one-two combination of the detective's glare and her mother rising from her chair to make her opinion heard. "Don't be ridiculous, Bailey. This garden party is your introduction with Harper as a couple to Kansas City society. I've taken Charlotte's eccentricities into consideration and scheduled it for one of those days when she's working at the museum."

Charlotte looked up at the handsome blond attorney with his hands resting on her stepsister's shoulders. "You're a couple?"

But her father didn't give either Harper or Bailey a chance to answer. "We've already discussed this. Detective Montgomery agrees that we need to maintain our regular activities so we don't scare off the bastard who wants to hurt my daughter."

Harper winked at Charlotte, but addressed himself to her father. "It was my suggestion, Jackson. Charlotte and I are friends from way back. Plus, Bailey was concerned."

Kyle spoke up from the buffet, where he was pouring himself a cup of coffee. "I agree with Bails. This party is a frivolous expense we don't need right now."

"I was worried about Charlotte, not the expense," Bailey insisted.

"I am, too." Kyle rejoined them at the table. "We don't need the distraction of any more people around the estate right now, do we?"

"Thanks, guys." Charlotte smiled at Kyle and squeezed her stepsister's pale hand. Bailey was quickly losing her rosy-eyed view of people—no doubt starting to feel like a pawn in the powerful man's world her mother had married into. And while Harper was saying and doing all the right things a solicitous boyfriend would, Charlotte got the idea that he was more focused on impressing her father, or even Detective Montgomery, than he was Bailey.

A decade had seasoned Harper's lanky good looks into a man who would turn any woman's head. With his family's reputation and bank account, he was definitely what society would label a catch. But as Charlotte studied his manicured hands and polished speech, she began to wonder exactly what it was that had made her think he was the god she'd crushed on so badly in high school.

The man standing in the archway had mud on his city-issued uniform and a scowl on his face. But she wasn't feeling so much as a flicker of interest in Harper this evening, yet Trip Jones stirred something deeper inside her.

True, she was a different woman now than she'd been in high school, before the kidnapping. Maybe that was the difference—Harper, while he cut a handsome figure in his tailored suit, seemed stuck in that boyish tendency to want to please anyone he perceived as more powerful than he was. Trip, to an annoying degree at times, didn't answer to any man or woman in this room. No one would ever mistake his brawny build and attitude as that of anything other than an intelligent, self-assured, full-grown man.

Those green-gold eyes were on her now, questioning her lingering perusal. But she felt no panic. There was something deep and intimate about the way he looked at her that thrilled a secret part of her that had been shut off for too long. Trip Jones was a man. He cared about her. He'd made no bones about the fact that he was attracted to her, that he wanted her in ways no man ever had before. She… believed…there was a bond growing between them that had nothing to do with stalkers and nightmares and keeping her safe. It was pretty heady stuff for an eccentric plain Jane to process.

No high-school boy had certainly ever looked at her that way. No high-school boy had ever kissed her or held her or sheltered her the way Trip Jones…

Charlotte snapped back to the conversation around her.

No high-school boy…

It couldn't be.

She interrupted the discussion. "Harper, do you ever hear from your soccer buddy Landon Turner?"

"That's a name I haven't heard in a while."

Her father curled his fist around the top of her chair. "It's a name I never want to hear in this house again. Sweetie, why don't you go to your rooms. Let us sort this all out."

Trip took a step into the room backing her up. "She needs an answer to her question. Do you know what Turner is up to these days?"

Harper shrugged and smoothed his tie. "To be honest, we lost track of each other in college. I was at Harvard and…I don't think he got to play professional soccer the way he wanted. He was a scholarship student at Sterling Academy in the first place, otherwise, he couldn't afford it. And with all the delays and backlash from your trial, he lost his full ride to Westminster. I think he ended up at the university, or maybe even a community college. We ran in different circles by that point. I'm afraid I lost track of him."

That could explain the drinking and the endless phone calls alternately blaming her for ruining his life and asking her forgiveness. But had Landon outgrown his troubles and moved on with his life? Or had he somehow snuck back into hers, intent on taking the absolution she hadn't been able to give.

And if he had slipped back into her life somehow, could he have changed his appearance so much that, after ten years, she no longer recognized him? Was he here right now? Watching her?

A ripple of unease shimmied over her skin, battling with the anticipation she felt at finally having some plausible answers to identify the man playing this cruel game of terror with her. But she couldn't think here, she couldn't handle another minute of people and arguing and feeling so exposed like this. Charlotte pushed her chair away from the table and stood. "If you'll excuse me. I need to go."

"Of course, sweetie." Jackson hugged her tight.

Detective Montgomery stood as well. "I'll call you if I have more questions."

With a smile for the others, she squished in her wet tennis shoes across the room to Trip.

"Did you need something?" he asked, his voice terse.

Charlotte opened her mouth to ask him to wait until they got to her rooms to explain the idea percolating in her head. But his arm went out in front of her like a crossing guard's, stopping her in her tracks, and she realized he was talking to the man leaning against the wall near the hallway that led from the dining room to the kitchen.

Bud Preston brushed the rain off the shoulders of his Darnell Events Staff jacket, tonguing that ever-present toothpick in his mouth. "I'm just the hired help, sir—moving furniture in the rain. Gotta love my job. You wouldn't begrudge a man coming in out of the rain to use the john, would you?"

Charlotte nodded toward the hallway. "There's a restroom back there you can use."

"Go." Trip's warning was short and sweet.

Jeffrey Beecher walked in behind Bud, pulling off his clear plastic raincoat and tugging down the sleeves of his suit jacket. As soon as he saw his man standing there, he huffed with disgust. "Preston. Get back to work. I need all that iron garden furniture unloaded from the truck. And stick to the floor runners when you come inside so you don't track your mess through the house."

Bud turned and gave his employer a mocking salute. "Sir, yes, sir."

Trip's arm dropped once Bud disappeared into the kitchen. Jeffrey pulled a handkerchief from his pocket and removed his glasses to wipe them dry. "Sorry about that," he apologized. "Have they finished dinner yet? I have some details I need to go over with Mrs. Austin-Mayweather." He paused when he met them in the archway, putting on his glasses and wrinkling his nose when he saw the muddy streaks in Max's fur. "Did something happen?"

Trip slipped his arm behind Charlotte's waist and scooted her on past without answering. "Join the party. We're out of here."

As soon as she'd turned all the locks on her door behind them, Charlotte hung her wet coat in the closet. While Max trotted on past her to get a drink of water from his bowl, she untied her wet shoes and peeled them off her feet. Her socks came next. She peeled them off and dropped them on the rug as she hurried straight to the bookshelves across the room.

She heard the rip of Velcro as Trip removed his vest, but she forgot to even offer him a seat as she pulled out her high-school yearbooks and curled up on the couch with the stack of books beside her. While she warmed her toes beneath her legs, she opened up the first yearbook and scrolled through the pages.

A lamp turned on beside her, showering more light over her shoulder. "What are you doing? I figured you'd head straight to the shower."

She glanced up at Trip and back to her book. "You can use it if you need to. I wanted to look something up."

"I can wait until I can get back to the station or my apartment for some clean clothes." Her balance shifted as the sofa took his weight beside her. He picked up another book and thumbed through the pages. "High-school yearbooks?"

Charlotte nodded, finding the section of photos she needed. "Something that creep said. That none of us would ever say no to him again."

"I don't follow."

She trailed through the senior class photos with her finger, going down the alphabet. "I've only said no to two guys my whole life. One of them was Landon Turner when he asked me to forgive him for pulling that prank on prom night. And the other..." She squinted to be sure, then pulled off her glasses and held the page up to her eyes to see the long-forgotten face once more. "There. Donny Kemp."

Trip was a blur at this distance. "Your brainiac friend from the quiz bowl team?"

She tapped the photo as she handed him the book. "I turned him down for a date to the prom, and went with Landon instead." Turning him down for a date wasn't much of a reason for a man to threaten her like he had, but her choices for men she'd wronged were limited. "I have no idea if he still lives in Kansas City or what he looks like now. It's hard to picture him ten years older and probably looking a little less nerdy."

Charlotte nearly toppled over when Trip stood. When he strode to the door, she grabbed her glasses and hurried after him. "Where are you going?"

"Lock the door behind me. Don't open it for anyone but me."

"Trip?"

"I'm going to show this to Montgomery and have him track down Donny Kemp. Landon Turner, too. Maybe we can get his artist to age their pictures for us and see if you recognize one of them then."

"I didn't say Donny was the killer. He was always kind of odd, but sweet." She hugged her arms around herself, hating that her revelation only raised more questions instead of offering answers. "And who am I to describe anyone else as 'odd'? And Landon was so...devastated when he found out what happened to me. He blamed himself for me getting hurt."

"Don't expect any sympathy from me." His voice was tough, but his fingers were gentle as he brushed a curl of hair off her glasses and cupped the side of her face. "They're leads, Charlotte. Something a lot more tangible and sensible than just waiting to catch this guy when he finally attacks and praying I'm not too late to stop him."

"GET OVER HERE, YOU goofy mutt!" Trip shouted, as Max trotted past the slobbery tennis ball he'd been so excited about just a moment ago and started nosing around the ground at the corner of the fence where he'd been trying to drag something through the ivy and chain links since they'd first come out for a morning romp. Pulling his new KCPD ball cap over his eyes to shield them from the morning drizzle, he jogged after the determined pooch. He picked up the abandoned tennis ball and gave the dog a playful swat on the rump. "Hey. Leave it."

Charlotte wore a bright yellow cap to match the brightly painted sunflowers that covered her ears. He still didn't think there was a thing wrong with the badge of honor she carried on the delicate lobe the doctors had repaired, but if she felt more comfortable hiding the scar, then he was content to let that vulnerable imperfection be a secret shared between them. Her skin glistened with raindrops and healthy activity as she ran up beside him, making it hard to imagine her as the skittish, reclusive heiress he'd first discovered in a storage room at the Mayweather Museum. "Maybe it's a dead bird or ground squirrel that's gotten flooded out by the storms."

"Charlotte!"

She'd knelt down to shoo Max away and inspect the juicy temptation for herself through the fence. "I sure hope the farmers appreciate all this rain because I, for one, am getting sick and tired of it. I'm running out of dry shoes. Yuck." Her tone changed from curiosity to gross-out as she stood. "I don't want to touch it without gloves. I think Max has been eating it."

Trip squatted down to inspect what looked like a fragrant hunk of liver out of the garbage. Yeah, what self-respecting dog could resist that? He stood back up and handed off the tennis ball. "I've got my gloves in the SUV. I'll come around the other side to pick it up."

"Wait." She pushed the ball back into his hands. "You keep Max entertained—you've about got him tuckered out already. I'll go in and ask one of the staff to remove it. He doesn't usually get this much action when it's just me in the morning. I think he's having fun."

She was already heading toward the door. "All right. I'll dog-sit. But you come right back, understand?"

"Got it. Now throw the ball."

Trip hurled the tennis ball and grinned at Charlotte's delight in watching Max run after, then nearly do a backflip when the ball bounced off the fence and changed course. The door clicked shut behind her as she went into the house. Then he threw the ball again, purposely avoiding the corner with the meat.

It felt good to stretch out his muscles after sleeping on a couch that was entirely too small in a room that reminded him entirely too much of the woman sleeping in the connecting bedroom. Especially when a freshly washed dog had insisted on sharing the couch with him and his mistress didn't.

He pulled the ball from Max's mouth and scratched behind his ears. "You and I are learning to get along pretty well now. But I still prefer her curves over yours."

Max woofed a protest. Although his heart was willing, he really was getting tired. When Trip threw the ball this time, the dog pushed to his feet and loped after it.

He'd left Charlotte alone only for the hour it took him to drive to KCPD headquarters, where he could shower and get some fresh jeans in the locker room, and run upstairs to check on Spencer Montgomery's progress in running down her old high-school buddies. While Rafe Delgado had camped out outside Charlotte's door, refusing to let anyone—not even her stepsister, Bailey, with a late-night snack—enter, Trip had gotten Montgomery to share some information that was as unsettling as it was unexpected.

Landon Turner now lived in the small mid-Missouri town of Osage Beach, where he worked as a deputy with the sheriff's department and coached a prep league soccer team. A few calls by Detective Montgomery verified that Turner had not only been on duty in the Lake of the Ozarks area the past three days, but that he'd been on the scene of a multicar accident yesterday afternoon and evening when the RGK had been at the cemetery, spying on Charlotte's grief and paying an innocent man to help terrorize her with his van and a fancy flower.

As for Donny Kemp?

Trip wrestled with Max for a few seconds before tossing the ball again. At the same time, he was wrestling with exactly how he was going to share his suspicions with Charlotte.

While he took note of the dog's lethargy and waning interest in their game of fetch, Trip was more concerned about the best way to tell her that quiz bowl Donny seemed to have dropped off the face of the earth some five years ago. Montgomery had found no driver's license records, no tax statements, no prison record, no death certificate, nothing. Trip was a lot less wary of a man whose whereabouts could be accounted for than a man who'd simply ceased to exist.

As a law enforcement officer, Landon Turner could get access to the police reports and trial transcripts of Charlotte's kidnapping—right down to the last details that she hadn't even shared with him yet. Could Donny Kemp, if he was still alive, get his hands on the same information through another source?

A retching sound drew Trip's attention from his speculation. "Whoa, pal. Hey, you okay?" Max had stopped in the middle of the yard and was swaying back and forth as his stomach heaved in and out. Trip hurried to his side. "Serves you right for eating things that don't belong to you. You're not spitting up my hat you ate, are you?"

But when the dog stretched out on his belly and started getting sick again, Trip's teasing turned to real concern. "Easy, boy."

He didn't like the looks of the little pellets he could still see in the chewed meat. He laid a comforting hand on the dog's back and pulled out his pocketknife to remove one of the pellets. The thing crumbled into bits, but enough remained that he had a pretty good idea of what he was looking at.

"Son of a bitch." He wiped the blade in the grass and returned it to his pocket as the convulsions subsided. Although Trip had basic medic training to deal with human illnesses and injuries, he wasn't sure how much of that could be applied to canines. But rheumy eyes and another round of vomiting couldn't be good. If the Rich Girl Killer wanted to torment Charlotte, he couldn't find a crueler way than to go after her truest friend like this. "Oh, no you don't. Charlotte! Hey! Somebody!"

With a crummy sense of déjà vu, Trip unhooked the top buttons of his shirt and peeled the chambray off over his head. "Hang in there, boy. Hang in there."

He tore the sleeve from the body of the shirt and scooped up a sample of the meat and pellets. Then he wrapped the dog in the rest of his shirt, hoping the cooling temperature of his nose was due to the weather and not something more sinister. Weak as he was, the dog resisted the straitjacket effect of the shirt. "Easy. Come on, pal. I need you to be okay for your mama."

As he scooped the dog into his arms, the door from the house opened behind him and he heard Charlotte's sharp voice. "I'm sorry, Kyle. But it's not really yours to worry about, now is it?"

"I'm a professional money manager, Char. I'm just suggesting you show a little restraint."

"I know how to manage a budget, and I'm not spending anybody's money but my own...Max?" She was at Trip's side in an instant, her hands stroking the dog's head and calming him. "Maxie, sweetie, what's wrong? Oh, my God." She pulled her hand away from his muzzle with blood on her fingers. "Max!"

Trip didn't have a hand to spare to wipe that mess from her fingers or the time to give the words of reassurance that might erase the shock from her expression.

"Is something wrong with your mutt?" Kyle asked from the doorway, staying out of the rain and away from the trauma.

"Kyle! Towels, now," Trip ordered, not caring if it was a weak stomach or indifference that kept her stepbrother from helping out. Once he got Kyle moving, he stood, cradling the sick dog in his arms. He held out the smaller bundle in his hand and looked down at Charlotte's tearing eyes. Oh, no, no, no. This pooch had to make it. He wouldn't be able to handle Charlotte grieving over that loss. "You're not going to wimp out on me now, are you?"

"No." She tilted her chin and grabbed the sample without hesitation. "Tell me what to do."

She stayed right beside him as he carried Max to the door. "Get the keys to the SUV out of my front right pocket." They were in the house now, hurrying past a stunned kitchen staff. "Call your vet. Does he have an emergency room?"

"*She* does."

"Can you manage the dog and give me directions while I drive?"

"Yes." She took the towels from Kyle's hand as they passed the bathroom and quickened her step to wrap another layer of warmth around the dog. "What's happening?"

"I'm no expert, but I think he's been fed rat poison."

Chapter Eleven

Charlotte let go of Trip just long enough to step into the restroom and wash her hands. Then she was back in the tiny examination room, waiting for the vet to give her a report on Max's condition. Trip was her hero throughout the endless ordeal—from putting the siren on top of the SWAT SUV and getting Max to the E.R. in a matter of minutes, to never once complaining about her wringing his fingers off.

The hours of waiting were pure torture, but she couldn't be anywhere else right now. Max needed her. Sweet, silly, loyal Max, who'd already suffered through one disastrous prank, had been victimized again. Charlotte's hand drifted to her earring, reaching beneath it to touch the permanent mark of the violence she'd suffered—the mark that made her a kindred spirit with her beloved pet.

"That's why you chose Max, isn't it?" Trip's husky voice pulled her from her thoughts. He batted her hand away to tuck her hair behind her ear and trace his fingers around the delicate shell. "You both lost part of your ear because of someone else's cruelty."

Although his touch soothed, she squirmed away.

"You love him despite his flaws. In fact, I'd wager those imperfections are a big part of what makes him so special to you."

She tried to make a joke of it. "We're both a little shy of winning blue ribbons for our looks?"

But there was only heat and sincerity and maybe a touch of sadness in those verdant-gold eyes looking down at her. "You've both survived hell and know it's the beauty inside, the beauty you have to look for, that means something."

He threaded his fingers into her hair and dipped his head to kiss her ear. He was seeing her deformity. Touching it. She twisted her neck away. He didn't release her. After a patient pause, he brushed his warm lips over her ear again. "This is beautiful." She gasped at the ticklish contact and tilted her head. He hovered a few inches away, then kissed it again. "You're beautiful." This time she held her breath, held herself still beneath his healing ministrations, as he dragged his lips around the shell. She could only feel his breath teasing her scalp when he pressed his lips against the scar itself. "Max is lucky to have you."

"He's lucky to have you." She turned her head again, not to pull away from his touch, but to look straight up into his kind, caring, see-into-her-more-than-they-should eyes. "I'm lucky to have you."

His mouth curved into a rueful grin. "Hold that thought until we hear from the doc."

When he would have pulled away, Charlotte walked into his chest, seeking his warmth and strength. And for some reason she wasn't quite sure she understood, he wrapped his arms around her and gave them.

"He'll be all right, Trip. He has to be." She locked her arms behind his waist and snuggled beneath his chin. "He helped me get out of the house that first time. He helped me talk to you."

"Because the crazy mutt was eating my hat."

"No." She smiled at the understanding dawning inside her. "Because he wasn't afraid of you. Because you were kind to him, I knew you…were kind. Not a bully at all."

"Well, then, I owe him one."

For ten years, she'd thought of home as her sanctuary, the one place where she could feel safe. But knowing some coward was there, under the very same roof, who could harm an innocent creature like Max—and have no qualms about killing him—left Charlotte floating in a landless sea of doubt and suspicion. No *place* was truly safe, and any sense of security that locks and doors and reinforced walls had given her was false.

But she was holding on to an anchor right now

that gave her hands and her hopes something solid to cling to. Safety wasn't a place. It was a feeling.

What she felt for Trip, the love and trust that were growing inside her—the possibility he could be feeling some of that for her—*that* was the security she craved.

The only way to overcome her phobias was to deal with them, not hide from the things that triggered them. And the only way she could finally work her way past the craziness in her head was to take that leap of faith Trip had asked her to. It was up to her to prove to him—and to herself—that she could love and be loved.

But until she could figure out exactly how to do that, she'd simply hold on to Trip. For as long as he would let her.

A knock at the exam room door stopped her wandering thoughts. She quickly turned as the door opened and the lady vet walked in.

Trip's hand wrapped around both of hers. "Doctor Girard?"

The vet tucked her stethoscope into the pocket of her lab coat. "I have some good news and some bad news."

"Definitely the good news," Charlotte begged. "Please."

"The good news is—I think Max is going to be okay."

"Oh, thank God."

"Yes!" Trip scooped Charlotte up in his arms and lifted her off her feet, nearly crushing her with relief and celebration before letting her toes touch the floor again. "That's one stubborn dog. I wonder who he takes after."

"You, probably."

"Being as young and healthy as he is definitely helps," the vet agreed. "We got him the antidote within the twelve-hour time frame. He's still a little out of it, but he's resting now. He sits up in his kennel in the back room and looks at me every time I go to check on him."

Charlotte was almost light-headed with relief. "That's wonderful. May I see him?"

"For a few minutes. The main thing he needs now is rest and IV fluids to replace what he's lost. I'd like to keep him twenty-four hours for observation— just to make sure the toxin is completely out of his system and that there are no lasting side effects."

"Thank you."

When Charlotte hurried to follow, Trip's hand held her back. "Wait a minute. Doc, you said there was some bad news."

"Well, I suppose this is more for the police and animal control, but, after analyzing the sample from his stomach, I'm pretty sure this was deliberate." Charlotte's heart sank and her temper raged all at once. "For whatever reason, someone tried to kill your dog."

"YOU'RE SURE THIS IS what you want to do?" Trip dashed inside after Charlotte and closed the Mayweather Museum's steel back door. He swiped the rain from his face and hair, and paused to inspect the newly installed dead bolt. Once he was satisfied that the steel door was secured, he followed Charlotte into the warehouse with his toolbox from the SWAT SUV. "You don't have to talk to anybody at the estate if you want to hide out in your rooms. I'll make sure you're not bothered."

"That's the last place I want to be." She scooped up a handful of the yellow crime scene tape that had been cut down and tossed it in the trash can on her way through the museum to check the locks on the doors into the public area of the museum. "Wow, when Detective Montgomery said KCPD had cleared the scene, I guess I thought that meant they'd cleaned it, too. Look at those crates left open. And all this black dust?"

"The CSIs took a lot of fingerprints. All of them were excluded as ours or other museum employees. I'm guessing our guy wore gloves." No surprise there. Even one hint of DNA or a fingerprint and they'd have ID'd the RGK and put him away months ago.

Charlotte climbed over the table and the door to the storage room still leaning against it to look inside the room. She muttered a curse. "Nothing's been put away." She picked up one small box and set it back on a shelf. "Some of these items have lasted for centuries, but they won't last another day unless we take care of this mess."

He liked seeing her determined, excited, not thinking one whit about her fears, as she was now. While she might be trying a little too hard to stay busy to keep her mind off Max's near-death experience and their twenty-four-hour separation, Trip had a feeling he was seeing a glimpse of the woman Charlotte was meant to be. The one she would have been all along if greed and tragedy hadn't changed her life. This was the woman who chased dogs and climbed through the mud and kissed him as if she couldn't get enough of him when she wasn't too worried or frightened or overanalyzing things.

This was the woman he wanted—in every way a man could want a woman.

The boom of thunder overhead and the slapping sheets of rain and wind against the bricks from the storm outside shook him out of that sentimental vibe. Her mantra was to "stay in the moment." He'd be a better cop and a smarter man if he could remember to do the same.

The flicker of lightning through the windows high above them reminded Trip to double-check the switch box and electrical connections. If Charlotte was trusting him to bring her here and keep her safe, then he was going to ensure that every possible contingency for danger or panic was taken care of.

Bad guys. Blackouts. Food. Floods. He had it all covered.

She set their sack of takeout dinner on the concrete floor beside her backpack and peeled off her black raincoat. She sprayed another layer of droplets across the front of Trip's wet T-shirt when she shook the excess water from her hair. "Oops. Sorry."

"I'm learning to expect that my time with you won't be neat and pretty, and that there's a fifty-fifty chance I'm going to wind up getting hurt somehow."

"I don't do it on purpose, you know. I'm just…" She reached out to wipe the water away, but he was already wet through to the skin. And either she was suddenly self-conscious about touching the pecs and nipples he unintentionally had on display—or she was feeling the heated intimacy of being alone here together as fiercely as he was. She stopped just shy of putting her hand on him before curling her fingers into a fist.

"A klutz?"

Her gaze darted up to his. "I was thinking *distracted*." She smiled nervously and picked up the sack. "There are some paper towels in the bathroom next to my office. I'll go get some."

A few paper towels and some Chinese takeout weren't going to douse the hunger that had been gnawing at him since Charlotte had asked him to bring her here. For the first time since he'd met her, she'd asked to be alone with him. She'd said the only place left where she could feel safe was here at the museum...with him.

That was a far cry from the woman who'd come at him with a sword and a rebel yell. Tonight felt almost like her version of a date—as if she wanted to be alone with him.

"Down, boy."

Charlotte had told him she had next to no experience with men. Her idea of being alone with him might be very different from what his randy hormones were thinking. So, ignoring the storm simmering inside his veins, he checked the gun and ammo clip on his belt, rechecked the doors and followed Charlotte into her office.

Trip quickly discovered that "office" was a relative term. Charlotte's work space away from her sitting room at home involved a desk and computer, yes, but there were also bookshelves, a long table made of a sheet of plywood over two sawhorses, stacks of crates, a workbench fitted with brushes, small picks, magnifying glasses and other small tools, a cushy dog bed and a beat-up end table where she'd set up their dinner beside a distressed leather couch with a blue-and-white quilt thrown over it.

"You sure there's room for me in here?" he teased.

She motioned him over to the desk chair she'd rolled up to the table and curled her legs beneath her to sit on the end of the couch. "It's perfectly comfortable when I work here late and need to take a nap."

He scooted between the worktable and desk. "Yeah, but I'm twice as big as you are."

"So you'll make it cozy in here." She smiled and he was helpless to do anything but what she asked. "Sit. Eat. Because after I make a couple of phone calls, I intend to put you to work."

Forty minutes later, Charlotte was on the phone to someone at the bank while he called in his location to Captain Cutler. A check outside the door showed him the sky was black, some of the lights were out in the downtown district and the rain was showing no signs of stopping. The weather report concerned Trip almost as much as hearing they were no closer to tracking down the identity of the Rich Girl Killer. After hanging up, he locked the door, did a quick check of the premises and ended up leaning against the door frame of Charlotte's office while she politely argued with someone on the phone.

"Well, no, that doesn't make any sense. Please do. I'll go ahead and start the endowment paperwork with our attorneys, but I'll tell them the check will have to wait until I hear from you. Thanks."

"Problem?"

Charlotte closed her phone and jotted something on a notepad before answering. "I wanted to talk to the bank before they closed about setting up the college fund for Richard's grandchildren. I figured endowing the fund with five hundred thousand would be enough to finance the education of all six kids, and others, if they come along."

"Half a million? I'm lucky if I have enough money to pay all the bills at the end of the month."

"Apparently, so am I." She pushed the chair away from her desk and stood. A tiny frown between her eyebrows reflected her consternation. "When I said I wanted them to draft a check for me, they asked if I wanted to transfer funds from another account so I wouldn't go below the minimum balance Dad set up when I inherited the trust fund."

Trip tucked his fingers into the back pockets of his jeans and shrugged. "Five hundred grand is a big chunk of money."

"I don't mean to sound crass, but...not for me. Not for Dad." She worked her bottom lip between her teeth as she checked the numbers she'd written on the notepad. "I'm careful about how I spend my trust fund because this museum and a few select charities are really important to me. I don't want to make a promise to them and then leave them in the lurch."

He looked at the notes she showed him, but on first glance they were just a jumble of scratches and backward figures to his tired eyes. "And you're sure you've kept accurate records?"

"To the penny. My father didn't make his fortune

by not keeping track of the money he spends. And I learned from him." She tossed the notepad down beside her phone. "The bank is going to look into it."

"Have those attorneys look, too. Maybe someone at the bank has helped themselves to a little extra cash that they think you won't miss." Trip dealt with guns and bombs, protection details and hostage situations, not white-collar crime. "Larceny has never been part of the RGK's MO. He's about power and revenge, not money. So I don't think you need to worry that he's making some other kind of inroad into your life."

The wheels behind those intelligent eyes kicked into high gear. "You know, there have been a couple of anomalies with that creep coming after me. He wants me to feel the same fears I did when I was kidnapped, so he's recreated those events. The phone calls. The white van, the corsage. And Detective Montgomery said this guy had an obsessive-compulsive disorder—that he makes a plan and sticks to it, right?"

"What are you thinking?"

"I was never shot at during my kidnapping. No one stole any money from me. And no one poisoned a pet or hurt any animal I know of."

Ah, hell. Ah, double hell.

"There's more than one person trying to hurt you."

TRIP DIDN'T LIKE HIS next call to Michael Cutler any better than the first. With the possibility of not one, but two lowlifes out to hurt Charlotte, he'd agreed to put the rest of the team on standby alert. But with the spring deluge turning an overtaxed water system into the beginnings of a natural disaster, the captain had suggested that Charlotte would be safer if he kept her at the museum indefinitely, perhaps even through the night.

Trip opened his toolbox and then went to work replacing the hinges on the door he'd broken. He had the odds and ends he needed to piece it together well enough to rehang it in the frame until he could get to a proper hardware store. It was good that he had plenty to do to keep his hands busy.

Was he really worried about being cut off from backup? Not having the current stats on street closings if they needed to make a quick escape out of here? Or was he just antsy like a penned-up stallion at the thought of spending the night alone with Charlotte? Stretched out on that long, comfy couch. Together.

And having to be a gentleman about it.

He'd better start getting used to the idea of folding himself into that little office chair, instead.

"If you check your watch one more time, I'm going to get nervous," Charlotte observed as she held the door for him and he screwed it into place. They'd worked long enough for their clothes to dry stiff and uncomfortably, and for her to get a smudge of dust across her cheek. "Or should I be nervous?"

"Don't be." He buzzed the last screw in with his power drill and let the rain and thunder outside beat down on his conscience and fill the silence for a moment. "Captain Cutler said KCPD and the city's road crew have closed more of the streets around here."

She tested the door, seeming pleased with his handiwork. "We knew that. That's why the curator decided keep the museum closed for the rest of the week. Driving around this side of downtown could be a little dicey until the weather breaks."

He removed the drill's battery pack and put his tools away. "Cutler also warned me that Brush Creek and some of the area's drainage ditches have topped their banks. The bridges will be out of commission soon. Maybe we should have rethought coming here tonight."

"This building is airtight to control the environment of the pieces on display. Unless we leave the doors and windows open—"

"Which we won't."

"—we're not going to get any water in here."

Her arms were hugged tightly around her waist, an indicator she was picking up on some of his worries, but she kept her chin at that determined angle. She was trying so hard to keep this evening as normal as possible that it made Trip miss the barking dog and ancient broadsword just a little. With one finger, he wiped the smudge off her cheek, then lingered near the soft curls of her hair. "Just know, we may be stuck here until the rain stops."

"As long as you and I are the only ones stuck here."

He twirled his finger into a wayward curl and tucked it behind her ear. "No one else will get in. No one will take you from me, I promise."

Charlotte's eyes widened behind her glasses. "Take me?"

Trip pulled his hand away, tamping down a Neanderthal-like burst of heat inside him. She so did not mean that the way his body reacted to it. He'd just made a slip of the tongue and, ah hell. "We'd better get back to work."

Thank goodness there were plenty of boxes to lift and tables to set aright—plenty of work to stretch his muscles and get himself too tired to think about Charlotte in any way other than her protector.

He was helping her put the shelves back into place inside the storage closet when she spoke again. "So I have to figure out who Donny Kemp is now?"

Right. Keep talking about the case. "He's Montgomery's main suspect."

She stretched up on tiptoe, lifting a padded box packed with an assortment of stone knife blades and arrowheads. "I don't think I've even seen him since the kidnapping. It's not like I go to class reunions."

Trip took the box and set it on the top shelf over her head. "If it's him, he's changed his name. That probably means he's changed his looks, too. Maybe by something as drastic as cosmetic surgery—maybe just by growing a beard or dying his hair or wearing colored contacts."

The scents of rain and ancient stone and Charlotte stirred in his nose as she faced him. "But all I did was turn him down for a date. And I'm guessing I paid more for that lapse in judgment than he did."

"Maybe something else happened to him that you've forgotten, or didn't know about because you had the kidnapping and trial to contend with." Trip moved out of the closet, unable to find another way to curb the urge to tunnel his fingers into her hair, to dip his tongue into her sweet mouth and consume her, when he should be thinking about nothing else but keeping her safe.

"I'm calling Audrey. Maybe she can remember something about Donny. Although I still can't imagine how a computer geek can turn into the Rich Girl Killer."

He jerked at the soft touch of her hand on the back of his arm. Yeah, that was the way to get past this crazy desire. Put *that* look on her face.

While Charlotte hugged herself and turned toward her office, Trip waited to follow. "We don't have to understand the how and the why right now. Let's just see if we can find the guy. Call Audrey."

"AND YOU'RE SAFE?" Audrey asked.

Charlotte peeked over her shoulder at the man sitting on her office couch reading a book. The white T-shirt and worn jeans that hugged every hill and hollow of his powerful body, along with the work boots and imposing black gun he wore on his belt, seemed so at odds with the thick paperback and sternly focused eyes.

His big hands made the book look small, as if it was a fragile thing he was handling with great care. Trip was such a physical being, too big for her cramped, intellectual's office, maybe too big for her untested heart and the curiously powerful need she had to be close to him. Yet she knew he would show the woman he cared about the same diligent attention and reverent care that he showed that book.

When she felt the blush heat her cheeks, she turned back to the phone. "Yeah. There aren't many people out in the city tonight. Dad's the only one at home I told that I was coming here. And Trip's with me."

"Then you're safe."

"I know." Although they'd talked through dozens of possibilities, nothing had brought them any closer to identifying who their former classmate Donny Kemp had become. But by putting their heads together, they'd come up with a disturbing pattern that left Charlotte more and more convinced that he was the Rich Girl Killer. "You're sure about Val not hiring him at Gallagher Security?"

"Once you started asking questions, I remembered her saying that. He didn't pass the company's psych eval."

"Go figure."

"Yeah. He thought he could use their old school connection to guarantee himself a vice president's job, but Val said he gave her the creeps. That fits your timeline of him disappearing about five years ago."

"And you beat him out for the summer internship at Harvard?"

Charlotte could hear typing in the background. Her ever-efficient friend was probably transcribing this conversation with plans to show it to her boss, the district attorney. "I'm sure it was Daddy's influence as an alum that got me the position."

"Another example of an influential, wealthy woman keeping him from what he wanted. No wonder he hates us."

"He's disturbed, Char. There's nothing rational about terrorizing and killing us."

"I wonder how Gretchen hurt him." Unfortunately, with Gretchen's death, that would be a much harder connection to follow up on. "I can see him being heartbroken if she rejected him. But me?"

"Maybe Landon Turner wasn't the first guy the kidnappers approached about getting you to the dance." She heard some more typing, and a reminder from Alex in the background that it was late and they needed to get some sleep. "I'm going to do some more research into the men who abducted you. Maybe there's a link to Donny we haven't discovered yet."

"Don't do anything risky."

"With this guy hanging over me?"

"Huh?"

The next voice she heard was Alex's. "Good night, Charlotte."

She laughed. "Good night, Alex."

"Good night, shrimp," Trip hollered from the couch.

"I heard that."

There was a breathy interchange on the other end of the call that made Charlotte wonder which one of her friends had stolen a kiss. "Give me that."

Oh, to be so free and trusting with someone she cared about.

"Charlotte?" Audrey, apparently, won the struggle. "I can't wait until this is over and we can hang out again. I miss you."

"I miss you, too."

"If I get any brainstorm about where Donny is or who he's become, I'll let you know, okay?"

"Same here. Bye, Aud."

After hanging up, Charlotte looked through the window of her office into the shadows of the secured storage area. She felt oddly cocooned by layers of darkness and bricks and rain. She tried to summon the warning voices inside her head that normally sent her into fits of panic when she was away from home and something wasn't familiar to her. But the voices were sleeping. Or wising up. Home was no longer a safe place. The world wasn't a safe place. But here, in this room, on this night, with this man…

"Did you and Audrey solve all the world's problems?"

"Enough for tonight." She untied her high-tops and kicked them off on her way over to the couch. Tugging the quilt from the back of the sofa, she folded her legs in front of her, pretzel-style, in the opposite corner, hugging the quilt's softness in front of her. "So you think it's best if we stay put for the duration of the storm?"

He bookmarked his page with his finger. "Are you okay with that? With some of the streetlights out, I'd rather not risk running across any flash flooding in the dark. And I don't want to miss spotting an enemy before he sees us. But if you want out of here before daybreak, I'll find a way."

She shook her head with a smile. "I'm okay. This weather is just as dangerous for you as it is for me. So's…the other."

"I'll find a way," he repeated. She believed him.

"No. This won't be the first time I've slept here. Though, admittedly, it hasn't been through the night. Or, with a man." He gave her a look that pricked a riot of answering goose bumps across Charlotte's skin. But when he turned back to his book, the excitement faded and she tried to blame the electricity she still felt sparking through her on the storm outside. "What are you reading?"

He held up J.R.R. Tolkien's *The Return of the King*.

"Sorry, I was on the phone longer than I intended. I didn't mean to be distracting."

"You weren't."

"But you've only turned a couple of pages in the last…" Charlotte sank back into the cushions as she heard the incredulity in her own voice. "I'm sorry."

If he took any offense at her comment on the slowness of his reading, he didn't respond. Charlotte knew books, loved books. And when the uncomfortable silence between them continued, she began to talk books.

"Has Aragorn led his men against the gates of Mordor yet?"

With a huff of breath that seemed to fill the entire office, Trip tucked a slip of paper into his book and set it on the table beside him. He startled her when he spun in his seat to face her. "I don't want to read."

"Just tell me to shut up. I guess I am a little nervous about staying here all night. The last time I didn't go home, I was being held—"

He reached over, grabbed her foot and dragged her clear across the sofa, until her knee was wedged against his thigh and the quilt was the only thing between them. "I want to kiss you."

Charlotte's pulse thundered in her ears. "What's stopping you?"

"Don't want to scare you off."

"You really think *you* can scare me more than anything else that's happened this week?" She brushed her fingers across the masculine stubble of beard on his jaw, and the sea of goose bumps returned.

He slid his hands beneath her bottom and lifted her squarely onto his lap so that she straddled him, facing him. "Scared yet?"

"No." Although she was trembling, she braced her hands on his shoulders, waiting for the warning voices to kick in, to tell her she wasn't ready for this. But the searing heat gathering beneath her thighs and in between was saying something very different.

Trip pulled the quilt from between them and tossed it to the far end of the sofa, pulling her close enough that she could feel his body heat through their clothes, but the soft rasp of cotton knit rubbing against the wilting crispness of her blouse kept them apart. He lowered his head, his warm breath fanning across her skin, his eyes targeting her mouth. "Scared?"

She slid her hands behind his neck and up against his golden-brown hair. "Not of you. Not of this."

He rested his forehead against hers and inhaled a deep, stuttering breath. His eyes were still on her mouth, his hands were roaming with aimless, grasping friction up and down her hips and back. "Cripes, honey. I want you. I want all of you."

His strong thighs were wedged between hers, leaving her open and vulnerable and aching to be filled. Charlotte felt her temperature rising from the inside out, or perhaps it was the outside in. She only knew there were sparks of lightning and swirling storm clouds of need building in the tips of her breasts and every pore of her skin. And Trip wasn't kissing her yet.

"Trip," she begged. "Please."

"I never want to do anything that makes you look at me with fear in your eyes again. That tears me up inside. I'd rather take a bullet than see you crying or afraid of me again."

In the raging awakening of desires denied and put on hold for too long in her life, a surprising voice of compassion whispered to her. He'd admitted, not that long ago, that she had the power to hurt him. Joseph Jones, Jr., might be big, bad and bossy on the outside, but inside, her brawny protector had a weakness. And if she'd hidden away from the world for ten long years because she'd felt too weak to face her fears, why should she expect Trip to willingly risk what frightened him the most after only a week?

Charlotte rose up on her knees and took Trip's

face in her hands, looking him straight in the eye. "I'll tell you if I want you to stop, all right? If I get scared for even one moment—you'll stop?"

"Yes." Those eyes never lied.

Neither did hers. "Don't stop."

Trip closed his mouth over hers, tunneling his fingers into her hair to hold her lips against his when the force of his kiss pushed her away. Charlotte wound her arms around his neck and held on, opening her mouth to every foray of his tongue, welcoming his every touch.

When holding each other close wasn't close enough, Trip fell back across the sofa, pulling her on top of him. He kneaded her bottom, branding her through her jeans. Then his fingers slid higher, finding their way beneath her blouse, their calloused exploration striking heat against her cool skin. Her breasts pillowed against his harder chest, the ache in them eased by the contact, then stoked again as his hands began to move her up and down his body, creating a slow, delicious friction fueled by fiery kisses along her jaw and throat.

She was trapped in a torrent of hands and hardness and kisses and heat, with no outlet to ease the storm building inside her. Pressure gathered and heated in the heavy dampness between her thighs. And when her aching need fell open around the treelike hardness of Trip's thigh, she instinctively squeezed and rubbed, desperate for the release his body promised.

"Easy, honey," he rasped against her damaged ear, tenderly running his tongue around its delicate shell, arousing nerve endings that had never been touched this way before. "Easy."

As Charlotte moaned with frustrated need, he sat up, spilling her into his lap. He kissed her swollen lips, apologizing for the unwanted distance between them. His fingers moved to the buttons of her blouse, freeing the top two before peeling the whole thing off over her head so that he could pull her close and kiss her again.

Now she understood. He was delaying what she wanted, not denying her. A quick study in any subject, Charlotte reached for the hem of his T-shirt and tossed it to the floor beside her blouse. While he unhooked his belt and carefully removed his gun and badge to set both carefully within arm's reach on the floor beneath the sofa, she explored the responsive gasps and moans she elicited when she smoothed her palms across his taut male nipples, pinched one between her thumb and finger, eased its torment by laving it with her tongue.

"Charlotte," he growled with pleasure, flinching when she tasted the other nipple, shifting beneath her and letting her feel that he was just as powerfully aroused as she was. His hands moved to the clasp of her bra. "Careful what you ask for."

When the bra disappeared, he covered her with his big hands, squeezing, flicking his thumbs across each pebbled tip, testing the weight that seemed to grow heavier with every caress. Each touch sent a pulse of electricity straight to her weepy thighs. And when he closed his hot mouth over the first hard tip, she cried out his name as a lightning bolt of pure, raw heat sparked deep in her core.

"Trip?" Even as she clutched her fingers behind his head and held his mouth against her to ride out the exquisite torment, she was squirming, seeking, struggling to find that ultimate release his hands and mouth had primed her for. "Trip," she groaned.

"I know," he murmured against her breast. "I know, honey," he whispered against her ear. "I know."

He reclaimed her mouth in one hard, quick kiss and then put his skilled hands to use, deftly removing the last of their clothes, spreading the quilt beneath them, lying back on the sofa and stretching her on top of him. She nibbled at the edge of his square, unshaven jaw, marveled at the textural differences between her smooth legs and his harder male thighs, worked through an odd blend of excitement and trepidation at the pulsing length of his arousal nudging against her hip—as he pulled a foil pouch from his wallet and tore it open.

"I'm not on the pill or anything," she admitted, holding her breath and tilting her face up to his, worrying that he might have forgotten he was her first. Trying not to listen to a very old voice that tried to tell her she was plain and brainy and flaky and not the type of woman that a man like Trip would really—

"Shh." He hushed those doubts, twirling a wild curl around his finger and smiling as if he thought it was the most beautiful thing in the world. "Are you having second thoughts?"

She shook her head. "I never thought I'd be doing anything like this...that I'd want to. But I do."

He pulled her up to his mouth and kissed her softly, tenderly. "I'll protect you in this, too, honey. Trust me."

Charlotte had no idea how many pounds of strength and power were lying tightly leashed beneath her. But she wasn't afraid. This was right. Out of all the craziness and terror in her life, she knew this one thing was right. "I do trust you, Trip. I do."

Several slow, deliberate kisses later, and the storm was brewing again. Trip had sheathed himself and rolled Charlotte beneath him. He took the bulk of his weight off her with his elbows and entered her in one long, deep stroke, holding himself still inside her. Squeezing her eyes shut against the initial pain, the initial shock of this ultimate expression of intimacy and trust, Charlotte held her breath.

But he stroked her face, kissed the swell of her

breast, kissed her lips, waiting with tender patience for the pain to pass, for her body to adjust to his size, for the pressure to build to an almost unbearable mix of frustration and anticipation. "Trip, please." She was feverish, panting, ready to burst. "Please."

"Look at me, Charlotte." He took off her glasses and set them aside, making one request of her. "I need to see your eyes."

She opened them wide, looked up into the purposeful determination and caring light she saw in his gaze. Trip nodded and began to move inside her.

And when the love and need became too much for her heart and body to bear, she wrapped her heels behind his thighs and buttocks, wound her arms around his shoulders and covered her body with the weight of his. With the roar of his release, he unleashed the storm inside her and pleasure rained down around them both.

Chapter Twelve

So the eccentric brainiac with the ear-piercing whistle had some distinctly feminine wiles lurking inside her, after all.

It was a dangerous one-two punch straight at Trip's heart that he was still mulling over as Charlotte nestled closely to his side and snored softly against his chest. She'd made herself as vulnerable to him as a woman could be, giving him the gift of her body and her passion. She'd been so curiously eager, yet so achingly innocent—bold and giving and…trusting.

Twice.

He brushed the toffee curls off her forehead and bent his head to press a kiss to the crown of her hair, grinning at the innate spirit of adventure that Kansas City's most reclusive heiress had unbottled these past few days he'd known her. An hour after he'd exhausted himself making her first time as perfect for her as he knew how, she'd nudged him awake, whispered a request into his ear, climbed onto his lap—and he hadn't been able to resist her.

He couldn't imagine two more different people than him and Charlotte. Yet he couldn't imagine being without her now.

Feeling her shiver in her sleep, Trip pulled the quilt up over her naked back, snugged her more tightly in his arms and listened to the storm quieting into a steady rain outside. The past few hours had been perfect moments sliced out of time. Isolated from the rest of the world, with thick walls and heavy locks and the weather itself keeping the danger stalking her temporarily at bay, they could talk and cuddle, read to each other and make love. The two of them together could work.

But what about life outside these walls?

What about when his job took him out on a late-night call to any corner of the city? What about when he wanted to take her out and introduce her to his friends and she was so terrified of the outside world that she wouldn't leave her rooms or this museum? What about when her father compared her PhD with his community college degree, or her trust fund with his government paycheck?

Once the Rich Girl Killer was caught and he knew she was safe, how did Miss Charlotte Mayweather and Officer Trip Jones work?

He wasn't smart enough to have the answers yet. He only knew that he'd give his life for this woman.

She deserved to feel secure in her world and live whatever life she chose to lead.

And he'd give her his heart. If that was what she wanted.

Yeah, she already had that.

If.

THE CELL PHONE ON the desk was ringing.

Trip awoke, instantly alert, instantly aware of Charlotte's distress as she moaned and squirmed against him in her sleep.

"Make it stop," she murmured.

"Charlotte?"

Something wet and warm stung his skin. Ah, hell. She was crying. She was dreaming some damn-awful nightmare and she was crying.

Trip sat up, pulling her into his arms and gently shaking her awake. "Charlotte? Wake up, honey. It's a bad dream."

"Stop. Make it…"

The phone rang again and suddenly she was awake. She pushed her hair off her face and tugged the quilt up over her breasts. Her eyes were narrowed, searching, as if she was disoriented and surprised to find herself naked, her body tangled up with his.

"Charlotte?" *Please don't be afraid of me. Please don't regret what happened. Please don't give me that look.*

She whirled around as the phone continued to ring. "What time is it? Where are my glasses? Is that him?"

"Right here." He handed her her red glasses, scooted off the sofa and picked up his shorts as he looked at the phone. "It's almost three in the morning. Here."

He handed her the phone and she shied away. "Is it him?"

Trip shook his head. "It says 'Kyle.'"

"Kyle?" Her fear transformed into shock. Her posture relaxed and she reached for the phone, verifying the same name he had read. "Why on earth would my stepbrother be calling me at this time of night?"

Trip quickly dressed and rearmed himself with his Glock and spare 9 mil magazine, not liking the snippets of conversation he could hear on this end of the phone.

"Where? Brush Creek Boulevard and Hazelton. Got it." Trip laid out her clothes and politely turned his back as she followed his lead and got dressed. "Why did Harper let her leave by herself? I'll see what we can do from here. Yes, I'll tell him."

As soon as she set the phone on the desk beside him, Trip turned to see her zip up her jeans and, button by button, cover up those beautiful curves and the memory of how responsive they'd been to his every touch. He hated the grim line of her mouth that was still pink and swollen from the abrasion of his five o'clock shadow and hungry kisses.

Something was seriously wrong in Charlotte's world and Trip didn't waste words. "What is it?"

"Apparently, my stepsister, Bailey, was out on a date. She was driving home in this weather and her car stalled out crossing a flooded street." She sat to pull on her socks and red tennis shoes. "Either she's trapped in her car because of the water or she's scared to get out because of the neighborhood and the blackouts—I don't know. He said she was pretty upset and hard to understand."

"She should call 9-1-1."

Charlotte tied her second shoe and stood. "Kyle did."

Trip blocked the door. "Then what does he want from you?"

"It's only a couple of blocks from here. We can get to her before the emergency vehicles or Kyle can. At least keep her company until help arrives."

"*I* can keep her company. You're staying put." He left the office, pulling out his own phone. "Give me the address. As soon as I phone this in to Captain Cutler, I'll go."

"She's *my* sister." She quickened her pace to hurry after him. "Trip, think about it. It's the middle of the night, she's wrecked her car, she's all alone—you might be a little...scary."

"Wrong choice of words."

"On first impression. I meant what I said before. I'm not afraid of you now. Damn it, Trip." She grabbed his arm and asked him to stop and face her. "Are you telling me you didn't change your mind about me, too?" She had him there. "You're probably still not too sure when I'm going to wig out on you next, are you?"

"You're right. With you, I never know what to expect. I just know it's going to be interesting." He liked the idea of leaving her alone and unprotected a little less than he liked the idea of her being out in the open with him, anyway. "Put on your coat. And this."

He pulled the Kevlar vest from the hook where it had been drying and strapped it around her chest and back.

"We'll make this as quick as we can. You stay right beside me and do whatever I say the moment I say it. You're still my first priority, understand?"

She nodded. Smiled. Tugged on his shirt and pulled him down for a quick, surprising kiss. "Thank you. For everything."

THIS WASN'T RIGHT. Where was the damn dog?

He moved to a different position on top of the Mayweather Museum's roof and used his scope to follow the couple hurrying hand in hand through the rain. He sat back for a moment, needing time to sort things out.

His plan was to shoot both the bodyguard and the dog. Then Charlotte would be easy to take. She'd trust him dressed like this. With her boyfriend on the ground, bleeding to death, she'd be happy to see him.

He went back to his original position and scanned the back of the SUV. Had they left him there? Was the dog inside the building? It would be easy enough to get inside again, but that would mean changing his plan, altering his timetable. And he was ready to strike. Tonight. His hands itched with the need to close around Charlotte's throat.

But he'd always been so careful about his plans, so precise. He couldn't stand details that were out of place.

But the opportunity was here. The time was now. She'd be all alone.

He released his breath, calmed every muscle, picked up his duffel bag and followed.

TRIP WAS SOAKED TO the skin and feeling like a rookie again. When Captain Cutler and Sergeant Delgado and even that gung-ho newbie, Randy Murdock, arrived, they'd call him twenty kinds of fool for walking into an exposed, indefensible scene like this one.

If someone wanted to ambush Charlotte, this was the perfect setup. It was a lot easier to be seen than to see from this vantage point. Abandoned streets.

No lights for two city blocks. High-rise hotels on one side of the creek and adjacent roadway, two- and three-story shops and apartment buildings on the other—with plenty of open space in between where anyone with bright lights and a four-wheel-drive transport could reach them.

"Are you sure this is Bailey's car?" he shouted over the roar of Brush Creek hitting the concrete abutment on the underside of the Hazelton bridge and swirling past the silver sports car pinned between the bank and the bridge's outer wall.

"It looks like it. I don't know her license plate, though."

"Stay put."

He left Charlotte up on the road where the water was only ankle deep and waded into the rushing flood current with his flashlight. Testing each step to make sure he wasn't washed on down the creek, he approached the bobbing vehicle from behind, gritting his teeth against the abrasive sound of steel grinding against concrete. The water was pushing against his hips by the time he fought his way to the upstream side of the car.

"Is she in there?" He heard Charlotte's shout like a faint echo.

He shined his light inside the car. "No. It's empty."

He swung his light around, peering through the dimness of rain and shadows to see if he could spot any foot traffic on the sidewalks or streets. Deserted. Dead. They were the only souls out on a night like this.

"Is there any way to know if someone else could have picked her up? Her boyfriend, maybe? What the…?" The feeling of dread turned to fury as Trip's light hit the floorboard beneath the steering wheel. He flipped the steel flashlight in his hand and busted through the passenger-side window.

"What are you doing?" Charlotte shouted.

His eyes hadn't deceived him. The two-by-four wedged beneath the accelerator told him this was a trap, that the wreck had been staged, that the woman he loved was in mortal danger and he might be too late to keep her safe.

He plunged toward the higher ground, waving Charlotte back to the apartments across the street. "Get back to the sidewalk! I want you out of sight right now!"

"Trip?" She was frightened by his warning, but she was moving.

He stumbled once in his haste to get to her and swallowed a mouthful of gritty water. He spit it out and floated a few yards off course before he found his feet again. "Call your sister right now."

She had her phone out, was dialing. "Now you're scaring me."

"I don't think anyone went into the water in that car. It's a setup. Move."

It *was* a setup. Only Charlotte wasn't the target. Yet.

Trip spotted the subtle movement in the darkness on the roof of the apartments. He angled his light and caught its fleeting reflection off the lens of a rifle scope. "Run! Get back to the museum! Don't stop until that door's locked behind you!"

He reached for his gun.

But the bullet tore through his shoulder and knocked him back into the rushing water before it ever left his holster.

"Trip!"

Stay in the moment. Stay in the moment!

Charlotte stood frozen long enough to see him disappear beneath the surface of the water and for something darker to bubble up in his place. Blood? Oh, God.

"Trip!"

Rain smudged her glasses and tears blurred her vision, leaving her blind to the buffeting assault of noise around her—racing water, drumming rain, distant footsteps, her pounding heart. She needed Trip. Needed to get to him. Needed to help.

What the hell was going on? Was that a gunshot? Was Trip hurt? Was he dead?

She swiped the water from her glasses and scrubbed the tears from her face. She took one step off the sidewalk. Took a second and a third toward the rushing flood. The grinding crunch of crushing metal grated against her eardrums.

Bailey's car groaned as the rising water freed it from the bridge and carried it silently downstream.

"Oh, my God."

The water had taken Trip, too. She was paralyzed with fear. Alone. In the open. Trip was gone and she was helpless.

People can change. You want to change. You can do something about it.

Trip's words from the day of Richard's funeral rang in her ears. For ten years, she was trapped and afraid—helpless to face the world. In the span of a week, a friend had been murdered, and her nightmares had become a real, living thing. She'd met a man, made love, fallen in love…and refused to lose him.

She could change. She had changed.

Trip Jones had her back. And, by God, she was going to have his.

She pulled out her phone. She could call his captain, Michael Cutler. They were already on their way after Trip's call. But she'd tell them to hurry. Hurry! Get SWAT Team One here—they'd know what to do. Only, she had no idea what the number was. Idiot. Call 9-1-1.

A doorway opened and closed in the darkness behind her.

Run! Don't stop!

"Charlotte? Charlotte!"

Someone was shouting her name.

Run!

Charlotte's body reacted even before her brain fully kicked in. She took off, moving her legs. She stumbled at first, and the weight of the Kevlar threw her off balance and she landed on her hands and knees in the flooding street. But just as quickly as the water soaked through the vest, coat and clothes to chill her skin, she pushed back to her feet. She lifted her heavy wet shoes and jogged, stretching her legs, picking up speed. And then she remembered she damn well knew how to run and took off— splashing, speeding through the dark and the rain.

"Charlotte!"

Don't look. Run.

One block. Two. Turn.

The floodwaters that covered the sidewalks grew shallow, then disappeared by the time she crossed the street to the Mayweather's back entrance. Her lungs burned. She was cold. She was scared. She skirted the Dumpster and entered the alley lot.

And skidded to a stop.

Her mouth dropped open, she was breathing hard. For one split second she flashed back in time.

White van. Danger. "Don't hurt me…"

She started to mouth the words that had haunted her since that fateful night ten years earlier.

But she blinked the rain from her eyes, blanked the memory from her thoughts. She stayed in the moment.

Yes, there was a van parked in the alley next to Trip's SUV. But it wasn't white. And the man climbing out of the passenger side and hurrying toward her wasn't her enemy. "Kyle!"

Charlotte ran forward to meet him. She threw her arms around his neck and hugged him, reassured to see the familiar face. "Thank God. Have you heard from Bailey? She wasn't in her car. Please tell me she got out okay, that she's someplace safe."

Kyle patted her back, then left a brotherly arm around her shoulders as he started to walk. "Bailey's at home. She's fine."

"Thank God. I was so worried. We need to get help, Trip's hurt. Someone shot him. I'm not going to believe he's dead. I can't lose him." She took several steps with Kyle, then stopped and twisted away from his arm as the initial rush of relief cleared and his words truly registered. "Wait a minute. Bailey's at home? Why didn't you call me? Trip risked his life to save her. Why didn't you call?"

Kyle's blue eyes squinted against the rain. "Someone shot your boyfriend? Lucky break for me."

"What?"

"Get in the van, Charlotte."

And then she saw the gun in Kyle's hand. And the bruiser in a security guard uniform sliding open the van's side door. Along with the uniformed man behind the wheel, they were all waiting. To take her.

"No!" She backed away, tried to run.

"Get in the damn van!" But rough hands grabbed her, kicking and screaming, picked her up off the ground and threw her inside. Once the door slammed shut, Kyle turned down the collar of his raincoat and sat on an overturned crate, facing her while his silent, oversize friend bound her wrists and ankles with duct tape. "You've already made this more difficult than it needed to be, so be a good girl and shut up."

When déjà vu should have kicked in at this recreation of her kidnapping, it didn't. She was too angry at her stepbrother, too worried for Trip—too different a woman from what she'd once been to not want to fight back. She was firmly in this horrid moment, and fought back with the only weapon left her. Her words.

"You're the copycat—the one who's been aping the Rich Girl Killer, trying to drive me over the edge into crazy land. Why?"

He pulled a handkerchief from inside his coat and wiped the gun dry. "You can't keep spending your money, Charlotte. Because it's not there. I haven't put it all back yet. And Jackson can't find out."

"This is about money?"

"Yes, damn it! Millions and millions of it. These

fine young men work for a friend of mine and are here to help me get what I owe them."

She flinched at the tearing of her wet skin beneath the tape. "How about asking for a loan, Kyle? Why resort to this? Why kill a man?"

"I didn't kill anybody. Yet." He slipped the gun into his pocket and pulled out a long scarf. "I'm just being resourceful. I thought I could take advantage of all your paranoia and the way you kept flipping out with this Rich Girl Killer after you. I asked Jackson to have you declared incompetent—to give me legal guardianship over your trust fund."

"You stole money from my trust fund?"

"It's called embezzlement, Char. I tried to live up to Jackson's faith in me, but all my investments went belly up. So since you never pay any attention to the family business, I took your money to hide the losses and repay the man these two work for."

She eyed thug one and thug two and got a pretty good idea of what was going on. "A criminal? You got involved in something illegal and lost Dad's money and stole mine to hide your mistake?"

Kyle tossed the scarf to the man with the tape. "But you keep giving it away like it's water. There's no more to give away, Charlotte, you crazy bitch. I can't afford to lose my job or Jackson's support."

"Or get on their bad side?" Thug one was wrapping the scarf between his fists. "You don't think killing me is going to turn Dad into your enemy?"

"Me? But don't you see the brilliant setup? The Rich Girl Killer is going to murder you. I copied everything he was doing to you—I intensified it by shooting at you when you were stuck in the middle of all those people, on display for the public and press. I poisoned your stupid mutt. It's all leading up to your death at the hands of a notorious serial killer. I'll be sure to say something nice at your funeral."

Should she tell him that the RGK's MO was to strangle a woman with his hands, not use a ligature like a scarf? "Did you kill Richard?"

"No." Kyle tapped the driver's seat in some unspoken signal. "But that day at his funeral, I saw how you reacted when he contacted you. I upped the ante by pushing you harder to crack."

"I'm saner now than I've ever been, Kyle. More grounded. Looks like you failed at that job, too."

Rage reddened her stepbrother's face and he rose up, swinging his arm through the air and backhanding her across the face and sending her glasses flying. Charlotte fell to the floor of the van, her mouth tasting like copper, her head ringing. "You crazy Daddy's princess. You screwed up your life, but I'm not going to let you screw up mine." Kyle glanced over his shoulder to the front seat. "I don't want to do this here. Drive."

"I can't."

"What do you mean?" Kyle moved behind the driver's seat.

Thug one took his seat on the overturned crate to spy out the front, as well. Charlotte spotted a blur of red and rolled toward them, praying they were her glasses. Victory. But as she put them back on her face, her success was short-lived.

"Run him down. We don't need any witnesses."

What? Despite the bonds on her hands and ankles, Charlotte scrambled to her feet to look through the windshield, too. Her heart sang and sank all at the same time.

Trip.

He was standing at the end of the alley, his chest heaving in and out with every breath, soaked to the bone. Blood was turning the left shoulder of his white T-shirt crimson. He stood with his legs braced apart, his right arm raised in the air, with his gun pointing straight at them.

"Drive, you idiot!" Kyle shouted, stomping on the driver's foot atop the accelerator. "He can't play chicken with a speeding vehicle and win."

The van kicked into gear. The tires spun on the wet pavement, then found traction and lurched forward. Charlotte tumbled to the back of the van, screaming all the way. "No!"

TRIP STARED DOWN THE VAN. His muscles were shaking after a swim and a run and the sudden demand to be still. His chest ached with every breath, and he was guessing the bullet that had hit his shoulder had nicked a lung as well. His left arm no longer screamed in pain, but hung numb and, for the moment, useless at his side. He never wanted to be this wet again. But the rain was a good thing. It had masked his approach, and the chill of it hitting his skin kept him awake, alert, when every drop of blood seeping inside and out was pulling him toward sleep.

His gaze drifted once to Kyle Austin—now he understood why he'd never liked that guy. But then he turned his attention back to the business end of things and focused all his attention on the driver. *That* was his target.

He'd seen the scuffle in the van, had raged at the knowledge that Charlotte was the one being harmed. But he knew his training, knew what he had to do.

One man alone didn't take on an entire army. Wounded and outnumbered, he'd be of no use to Charlotte if he charged that van. A smart warrior used his experience and his surroundings and whatever skills he could to obtain and keep his advantage.

He was the biggest, baddest cop on SWAT Team One—the immovable force who held his ground and intimidated his enemy. He had hands that he'd learned over the years were good for a couple of things—fixing what was broken, making what was needed, protecting what was right and loving a woman. Loving his woman.

"I've got your back, honey."

The tires squealed on the wet pavement. By the time the stench of burnt rubber teased his nose, the van was racing toward him.

Trip stilled his hand and squeezed the trigger.

"No!" CHARLOTTE SCREAMED as the van hurtled toward Trip. Milliseconds flashed by like eons. "Move!"

She heard a gunshot. The windshield cracked and the driver slumped forward. There was another gunshot and another.

"Get him out of there!" Kyle yelled.

The van lurched from one side of the alley to the other, careening off the bricks, narrowly missing a power pole. Every time Charlotte made it to her feet, she was thrown to the floor of the van.

"Get him!" Kyle had a hold of the steering wheel now, and Thug one tried to pull the dead driver out of the way. "You son of a…"

The van picked up speed. Charlotte was on her feet. Kyle turned the van straight toward Trip.

"No!" She hopped forward, then threw herself at Kyle's back, knocking him into the dashboard before he could get into the driver's seat.

The van veered to the right, Trip flew into the air and they slammed into the trash Dumpster and skidded to a crashing stop. Charlotte hit the floor one more time, but the Kevlar protected her from the crate and flying debris that threw her into the van's side door.

She was woozy for the first few seconds her world was still, her stomach roiling from the killer carnival ride. Her body was bruised, but as soon as her head was clear, she shoved aside the debris, ignored the moans of her stepbrother and abductors, and pushed open the side door and tumbled out.

"Trip?" She clawed at the duct tape, but it held fast. So she crawled to her feet and hopped around the Dumpster. "Trip!"

He was lying in the middle of the road, scraped up, bleeding. His leg was twisted at a grotesque angle, telling her it was broken. But he was alive. She saw his chest heaving for breath, watched him trying to push himself up onto his right arm, heard him groan in agony and fall back to the pavement. "Charlotte?"

"Trip."

As she fell to her knees beside him, she heard the screech of brakes and a trio of clipped, angry shouts.

"Get a bus here, now! Murdock, van! Sarge, I want those men in handcuffs, now!"

Charlotte leaned over her fallen hero to wipe the rain from his eyes, nose and mouth, and to press a gentle kiss to his scraped-up jaw. "I thought you were dead."

"Not yet, honey." Two long blinks and the fading

focus of his handsome eyes revealed just how badly he was hurt, though. His fingers brushed against her thigh and she reached down, taking his hand between hers. "Are you hurt? Did they hurt you?"

Three dark figures swarmed past her. "I'm okay. I'm scared again. For you. But I'm okay."

"Engine's off!"

"Drop your weapon!"

"Get on the ground! I said get down!"

"Go, captain—we've got it covered."

Michael Cutler was suddenly kneeling down on the opposite side of Trip, taking a quick assessment of his injuries and calling it in on his radio. "Officer down, I repeat, officer down. Gunshot wound. Vehicular strike. Where the hell is that bus?"

He immediately pressed his hand against Trip's shoulder, and Trip winced with a curse.

"Gotta stop the bleeding, big guy." The captain pulled a knife from his belt and reached across Trip's chest to slice the tape from Charlotte's wrists. "Are you hurt, Miss Mayweather?"

She shook her head. "Trip saved me. If they'd taken me away in the van…they were going to kill me."

Was the captain smiling? "I didn't think he'd let that happen." Then he was by-the-book serious again. "Open your eyes, Jones. Stay with me. I need a report."

Trip's eyes slowly blinked open. "Yes, sir."

Rafe Delgado knelt down beside Charlotte. "That looks like a bad break. We'd better not move him."

"You squeamish, Miss Mayweather?" Cutler asked.

"No."

"Good." He grabbed her hands and placed them over the bullet wound on Trip's shoulder, pressing them down the way he had. "Feel how hard I'm pushing? Keep that same pressure there—no more, no less." He shrugged out of a backpack and pulled out a first aid kit, ripping open a couple of giant gauze pads. "What's the situation, Delgado?"

Rafe reached down and braced Trip's other shoulder to keep him from twisting with the pain. "Easy, big guy. You know, you're supposed to jump out of the way when a vehicle comes speeding toward you."

Trip nodded. "If there wasn't a lady present, I'd be flipping you off."

"Sarge?" the captain prompted.

"Bus and backup are en route. We've got one dead body and two perps handcuffed on the ground. One of them tried to take out Murdock. He won't be fathering children for the next month or so."

"Ouch." Trip grinned, but his eyes were drifting shut again.

She felt his blood seeping through her fingers, tears burning in her eyes and spilling over. "Trip? Don't leave me now, sweetheart. Don't leave me."

With a jerky movement, he lifted his hand and wiped the tears from her cheek. "Don't do that, okay? That'll really kill me."

Then his hand flopped down against her leg and his eyes drifted shut. "Trip!"

"Get the blanket out of my truck," the captain ordered. "He's going into shock."

Trip murmured between his lips. "I got your back, honey. I told you I did."

"I know."

"I love you."

She knew that, too. "And you say I'm crazy."

Chapter Thirteen

Trip checked the clock on the wall and wondered how much longer he had to listen to Rafe Delgado and Randy Murdock debate who should be given the credit for arresting Kyle Austin and his surviving band of would-be kidnappers—SWAT Team One or Spencer Montgomery?

The persnickety detective had probably been hassling Charlotte with questions about that night at the museum. Was there any connection to the Rich Girl Killer beyond the obvious copycat crimes? Did she see who'd shot him? He hadn't. All he could identify was a man on the roof with rifle and scope—his guess was the RGK. His guess had become Montgomery's leading theory when the lab's ballistics check proved that the bullet the doctors had taken out of Trip's chest didn't match the handguns they'd taken off Kyle and his goons.

Who was there to protect her from Montgomery? Or family members and staff she shouldn't trust? Who was going to play fetch with her dog and keep her company in those lonely, isolated rooms where she didn't belong?

Nineteen hours. Nineteen hours without seeing Charlotte, and all these yahoos would tell him was that she was fine. That she looked good. That she'd asked about him.

He'd been through surgery, had been hooked up to this pulley contraption to keep his set leg level and elevated. His leg itched like crazy inside its cast, and the stitched-up holes in his left arm and lung ached whenever he moved too far one way or the other. The nurse had offered him another round of painkillers, but why would he want to be drifting in la-la land when he could be refereeing a conversation between these guys?

"Look, guys." Murdock and Delgado stopped their bickering and Captain Cutler set aside the magazine he'd been reading in the corner. "I appreciate you coming to check on me and all—"

Captain Cutler strolled to the bed. "The doctors say you're here for a week, that you'll be off for rehab for a good three months, and that you'll need light duty for another month after that. I figure you can man the dispatch desk or drive the truck for us."

Delgado scoffed. "Hey, that's my job."

"I'm losing my team by attrition here. I'm going to wind up bringing Kincaid back from paternity leave early or promoting someone new to the team, and I haven't got this one trained yet." He winked at Murdock.

"Should I be insulted?"

"No, you should leave," Trip suggested. "You should all leave."

"My point is…" Michael Cutler was a man used to giving orders, not taking them. From anybody. "You've been beat up pretty bad, big guy. I want you back on my team. But I want you in one piece."

Trip's frustration waned for a moment. These really were good people, good friends. "Are you being mushy with me, sir?"

A light flashed out in the hallway, and all at once there was a buzz of conversations and another couple of flashes, and altogether too much hubbub for a place where patients were supposed to heal and get some rest.

Michael Cutler squeezed Trip's good shoulder and grinned. "I don't do mushy. I'm stalling for time."

His friends stepped back as the noise outside in the hallway grew louder. Then a couple of familiar faces popped through the doorway. "Hey, shrimp."

Trip smiled as his best friend, Alex Taylor, came forward to shake his hand. "Good to see, big guy. I'm tellin' ya, if I'd have been there, you'd still be in one piece."

"Oh, so now you think you're funny?"

"I think you missed me."

"Settle down, you two." His fiancée, Audrey,

leaned over and pressed a kiss to his cheek. That explained the flashing cameras. Pretty heiresses who'd gone into hiding because a killer wanted them dead tended to draw a crowd when they went out in public. Trip tucked away the wistful thought of Charlotte and fixed a smile on his face. "We brought you a present." She turned to the door. "Okay!"

The scrabbling of paws on the hospital's slick linoleum floor might be the second-best sound he could have heard right then. "Max!"

The black-and-tan torpedo ran into the room and launched himself onto Trip's bed. "Whoa. Hey. Ow. Good to see you, buddy. We survived, you and me. We survived."

It took a moment to wrestle the mutt down to his good side, accept a friendly lick or two and then inspect the red vest he was wearing. "Certified Therapy Dog?"

Captain Cutler whispered an order. "And now, we leave the room."

Audrey clicked her tongue and took Max's leash. "C'mon, boy. Aunt Audrey is going to find you a snack."

One moment, his hospital room was in chaos, the next—it was serenely perfect.

"Hey, Trip."

Charlotte Mayweather stood in his doorway. Her beautiful hair curling around her face, her high-topped tennis shoes on and her eyes smiling, beautiful, behind her red glasses.

"Get over here."

She ran to his bed, was far too cautious about winding her arms around his neck, and gently kissed him. Screw that. He was hungry, he was needy, and his eyes were inexplicably tearing up. Trip snatched her around the waist and pulled her right onto the bed with him, claiming her mouth and pouring out his love and feeling with his one good hand that she was well and truly here with him and she was all right.

When he let her come up for air, she touched his cheek, wiping away a tear. She stretched up to press the tenderest of kisses against his brow. "Don't do that sweetheart. It tears me up inside to see you hurting."

She smiled wisely, gently throwing his one phobia back at him. "I'm okay, Trip. I just needed to see you. And now I'm okay."

"God, I missed you." He grabbed a handful of her jacket and pulled her close again, kissing her cheek, kissing her neck. Her hands were on his face and in his hair as she returned the assault, kiss for kiss. "I was so worried something would happen to you. KCPD arrested your stepbrother, but the RGK is still out there." He kissed her hair, kissed her ear. Stopped himself short. "Hey, look at these pretty little earrings." He pulled far enough away to look her in the eye. "They're beautiful. They fit your ear perfectly."

"It's the new me. You said I could change. And I'm changing." She turned in the bed, adjusting her position so that she could lie beside him, with her head on his shoulder and her hand splayed possessively at the center of his chest. "I'm not hurting anything, am I? I know I have an unintentional habit of—"

"No." He draped his right arm behind her back and claimed an equally possessive handful of her beautiful bottom. "Nothing hurts with you here like this." A moment passed before he frowned and asked, "How did you get here?"

He felt her smiling through the thin cotton of his hospital gown. "Audrey and Alex drove me."

"I meant, this isn't your home or the museum. You've got Max with you, but, you're out in the world." He pressed a kiss to the crown of her hair. "You okay with that?"

She nodded. "It's a little scary. I'm not ready to drive myself yet or dive into the Plaza crowd when they turn on the lights Thanksgiving night. But I'm fine. I knew my driver, knew my destination—and I was so lonely without you. Like I said, I'm changing. I feel stronger now. I don't want to be a shut-in anymore. I want to live. And love."

"That makes two of us."

They lay together for several minutes, and Charlotte's

bravery and simple willingness to break free from her mental bonds to be with him healed things inside him that no doctor could touch.

"I hear you've got some time off coming up," Charlotte finally whispered. "Any plans on how you're going to spend it?"

"Any suggestions?"

She snuggled closer. "How about going on an archaeological dig with me? Unless I uncover another King Tut, I'm guessing the press won't follow me into the middle of nowhere. And we'd be overseas, beyond the reach of Donny Kemp or whatever he's calling himself now."

"The middle of nowhere can be a scary place."

"Not with you around. Nothing is too frightening for me to handle when I know you'll be there to have my back."

"I always will," he promised.

"Digs can be pretty remote. It might be just you and me. Alone in a tent."

"Will it be dry there?"

"We can go to a desert dig."

"Please. One sleeping bag?"

"Yes."

Fantasies did come true. "Where do I sign up?"

"I love you, Trip." She pushed herself up to seek out his eyes. "I may be a little flaky around the edges, but I've never been a liar. I'm *not* too flaky, am I? I mean, not too much for you to handle, right?"

"I see myself as kind of a 'Charlotte Whisperer.' I got you out of that house, didn't I? Got you to stop attacking me with archaic weapons and kiss me instead." He leaned forward and touched her lips to prove his point. "I think I can handle you."

"Are you sure you want to?"

"You are one of a kind, Miss Mayweather." Trip smiled and pulled her close. "And you're all mine."

Epilogue

The man showed his identification to the guard, emptied his pockets of anything suspicious and signed the chart to be admitted to the visitation room at KCPD's Fourth Precinct detention center.

He walked past a young pregnant woman and the lowlife in the orange jumpsuit who was lecturing her across the table. Other than the guard at the door and the man he was visiting, they were the only people in the room. Good.

Once he spotted his quarry, he straightened his tie and lapels and headed to the table at the far side of the room. He slid onto the bench on his side of the plastic table and studied the weak-jawed coward sitting across from him.

"Who are you?" Kyle Austin asked. "My court-appointed attorney? You look like an attorney."

He reached beneath the knot of his tie, into the lining of his suit and from the underside of his watch, and calmly began assembling his gift out of sight from the room's security cameras.

"Hey, c'mon, man. I'm as glad to get out of that cell as anybody, but I don't know you."

"Really?" he finally spoke. Compulsion had cleared his mind, left him focused on his task. "I thought you claimed to know me quite well. That I served as some sort of inspiration for you."

He pressed the pad into the palm of his hand and glanced down at the drop of poison glistening off the sharp tip of the attached needle, carefully avoiding pricking his own skin.

His father and uncles had taught him well. They'd taken him all over the country, all over the world, to learn their craft. They'd beaten him senseless when he hadn't learned it right. So he was very careful, very correct, very precise in every task he set for himself now.

"Wait a minute, are you...?"

"I believe your stepsister knows me far better than you do."

"The RGK?"

He held out his hand and Kyle was already instinctively reaching across the table to shake his hand the way any man would. He took Kyle's hand, pricked his skin, held on tight when the other man flinched so he wouldn't waste a drop of the precious potion he was injecting into him.

Kyle Austin was already feeling the effects. His joints were locking up, his breath was constricting, his heart was stopping.

The visitor stood, pulling out his handkerchief to hide the device and wipe the trace of the other man's blood from his hand.

"Never interfere with a plan of mine again."

* * * * *

LARGER-PRINT BOOKS!

GET 2 FREE LARGER-PRINT NOVELS PLUS
2 FREE GIFTS!

Harlequin®

INTRIGUE®

BREATHTAKING ROMANTIC SUSPENSE

YES! Please send me 2 FREE LARGER-PRINT Harlequin Intrigue® novels and my 2 FREE gifts (gifts are worth about $10). After receiving them, if I don't wish to receive any more books, I can return the shipping statement marked "cancel." If I don't cancel, I will receive 6 brand-new novels every month and be billed just $4.99 per book in the U.S. or $5.74 per book in Canada. That's a saving of at least 13% off the cover price! It's quite a bargain! Shipping and handling is just 50¢ per book in the U.S. and 75¢ per book in Canada.* I understand that accepting the 2 free books and gifts places me under no obligation to buy anything. I can always return a shipment and cancel at any time. Even if I never buy another book, the two free books and gifts are mine to keep forever.

199/399 HDN FC7W

Name _____ (PLEASE PRINT) _____

Address _____ Apt. # _____

City _____ State/Prov. _____ Zip/Postal Code _____

Signature (if under 18, a parent or guardian must sign) _____

Mail to the **Reader Service:**
IN U.S.A.: P.O. Box 1867, Buffalo, NY 14240-1867
IN CANADA: P.O. Box 609, Fort Erie, Ontario L2A 5X3

Not valid for current subscribers to Harlequin Intrigue Larger-Print books.

**Are you a subscriber to Harlequin Intrigue books
and want to receive the larger-print edition?
Call 1-800-873-8635 today or visit www.ReaderService.com.**

* Terms and prices subject to change without notice. Prices do not include applicable taxes. Sales tax applicable in N.Y. Canadian residents will be charged applicable taxes. Offer not valid in Quebec. This offer is limited to one order per household. All orders subject to credit approval. Credit or debit balances in a customer's account(s) may be offset by any other outstanding balance owed by or to the customer. Please allow 4 to 6 weeks for delivery. Offer available while quantities last.

Your Privacy—The Reader Service is committed to protecting your privacy. Our Privacy Policy is available online at www.ReaderService.com or upon request from the Reader Service.

We make a portion of our mailing list available to reputable third parties that offer products we believe may interest you. If you prefer that we not exchange your name with third parties, or if you wish to clarify or modify your communication preferences, please visit us at www.ReaderService.com/consumerchoice or write to us at Reader Service Preference Service, P.O. Box 9062, Buffalo, NY 14269. Include your complete name and address.